Fibers

Jennifer-Crystal Johnson

Book #1 of the

Infiltration Trilogy

ISBN-10: 0692661301
ISBN-13: 978-0692661307

Written & Prepared for Publication by Jennifer-Crystal Johnson
www.JenniferCrystalJohnson.com
Published by Broken Publications
www.BrokenPublications.com

Cover Photography by Daniel Nattress
https://www.facebook.com/Hadley-Rae-Photography-120462984663755/timeline/
Cover model: Guenevere Cunningham
http://bit.ly/ArtLoverYT
Makeup artist: Malinda Ayers
www.MalindaAyers.com
Title Font: deRez by Foam Train Fonts
www.FoamTrain.com

Disclaimer:
This is a work of fiction. Names, characters, businesses, places, events and incidents are either the products of the author's imagination or used in a fictitious manner. Any resemblance to actual persons, living or dead, or actual events is purely coincidental.

Morgellons is a *real condition* that is yet to be cured. For more information on the real Morgellons disease, visit http://www.thecehf.org/. If you or someone you know has Morgellons disease, please consult your physician. Symptoms of Morgellons in this book are fictitious or used in a fictitious manner.

A
Pacific Northwest
Publisher

www.BrokenPublications.com

For my friend, Michael Adams.

Thank you for listening to all of my crazy ideas and consistently giving priceless feedback. I appreciate you letting me pick your brain on a regular basis! =)

For my daughters, Guen and Sonja.

You amaze me more each day with how much you understand and how entrepreneurial you are. Keep up the awesome work! I love you bunches =).

For my son, Gabe, who keeps me on my toes!

For my bestie:

I love you =).

Finally, for Mom and Dad.

Thank you for supporting me in my pursuits, which have never been ordinary or simple. Your belief in me has always been paramount to my belief in myself.

Acknowledgments

I have so many people to thank for their support and contributions to this book that I'm not entirely sure where to begin. However, there are a handful of names who stand out to me, and the first people I want to thank are those who volunteered to give me feedback on this work before publication and made it that much better.

Michael Adams, who has earned the title of Creative Consultant as far as my fiction writing is concerned, is a fountain of excellent questions, great ideas, and being able to help me tie everything together seamlessly.

My best friend & partner in crime, author Dalian Graylocke, whom I absolutely adore collaborating with because we're so different but so complementary. Love you!
http://daliangraylocke.weebly.com/

Author Tamela Miles, whom I worked with on a collection of short stories under Broken Publications and who graciously volunteered her time to tell me what she thought of this book. Thank you!
https://twitter.com/jackiebrown20

Author DL McKinnon, who also offered feedback on this first book of the trilogy while in the midst of working on his own creative endeavors.
http://www.author-mckinnon.com/

Next, I have to thank my family and friends for listening to me work through all the crazy aspects of this book, hear me ramble on about theoretical technology, and talk about real-life phenomena that absolutely fascinated me... so much so that this fictional series came to exist.

I would also like to thank my kids for taking such an active interest in my work as well as listening to me read excerpts when I got really excited about something. I love you! <3

Chapter One

Anna Reynolds didn't know it yet, but she was caught up in the middle of an interdimensional conspiracy. Her life seemed ordinary enough: a house, a job, a best friend, an SUV, and hardships in her past. She would soon discover a much deeper meaning to her existence that neither she nor her lively friend could have even begun to imagine.

"Hey, you," Anna said, flashing a bright, happy smile at her best friend. Though she smiled, her head was clouded with anxiety.

"Hey yourself!" Casey beamed. They embraced and took a seat at their favorite table, immediately ordering a bottle of wine.

"You wouldn't believe the crazy week I've had," Casey confided, decisively setting down her menu after just a couple of minutes. Casey Carlisle always knew what she wanted; sometimes she went a little overboard to get it, but she always *knew*.

Anna smiled, ready to hear all about her friend's crazy life to distract her from the strange events that had been plaguing her own. She couldn't deny it – Casey had a much more chaotic life than Anna did, but Anna was a loner at heart. She liked to be home, to be quiet and surrounded by peace. The rush and chaos of Casey's life fascinated Anna, but she appreciated that she only witnessed it from afar and didn't live it on a daily basis. She got exhausted just listening sometimes, wondering how in the world Casey did it all. Then again, she was younger than Anna by about seven years. Maybe that was why she had so much energy.

"So after the stupid cop pulled me over, she seriously accused me of not wearing my seatbelt. Twice! With all three of the kids in the car. And she was so rude about it that it made me hate that cops have any kind of power at all. I seriously wanted to punch her in the throat," she concluded, giggling. Anna had to laugh because she knew that Casey would never act on her violent ravings.

"Did she end up giving you a ticket?" she asked, wondering if Casey was really over it or just doing her laugh-to-hide-the-anger thing.

"Of course!" Casey exclaimed, feeding the fire in her eyes. "I'm contesting it on principle. There was absolutely no reason for her to be that rude to me or make unfounded accusations in front of my kids. She changed her story the second time she accused me, too, but that doesn't change the fact that it was a lie and she was digging for something else to give me a ticket for. Anyone who knows me can vouch that I wear my seatbelt to cross the damn parking lot." She paused, thinking about her kids. "I mean, what kind of idiot cop talks to a mother like that in front of her kids? The kids no longer respect the police. Jason asked me if cops are really the good guys after we left. She just did damage to years of trying to teach them that police officers are there to help!"

Anna knew her friend was upset about the incident, and for good reason. She agreed completely but wondered what kind of spiteful thoughts were running through Casey's head that shouldn't be.

"I'm sure the court will either toss it or lower the amount you have to pay. They don't usually keep people's tickets at full price if you go in and contest it."

"I know, and that's what I plan to do. I haven't decided yet, but I might write to the chief of police about his officer's disrespectful and unprofessional demeanor. That was just unacceptable." Casey sighed deeply and let her breath out slowly before changing the subject. "Okay. Rant over. How was your week? Anything exciting happen?"

Anna laughed. "When does anything exciting ever happen to *me*?" she asked, feeling a flash of guilt for keeping secrets from her best friend. "I lead a nice, quiet life and *you're* the excitement and drama in it," she added just as the waiter arrived. Smiling, he did his scripted spiel about the specials and waited for them to order. Casey went first while Anna still hadn't decided what she wanted.

"I'll have the T-bone steak, medium rare, and can you add some pepperoncini? I feel like a little bit of a kick." She smiled mischievously and handed the waiter her menu.

"I'll have the French dip with provolone," Anna said simply, also handing back her menu.

The two couldn't be more different, but they had some pretty important things in common. Casey was a single mom of three, surrounded by chaos constantly. She was a writer and entrepreneur, always looking for ways to make passive income. With little kids around all the time, it was anything but easy for her. Jason was six, Lisa was five, and Sally was three.

Anna had lost her son, Ezra, in a car accident six years earlier, so seeing Casey's kids was always bittersweet. He'd been on his way home from a soccer game in a carpool one evening when a drunk driver hit the van. Anna hadn't been driving; it was one of the other moms from the team. Anna still hated herself for not being the one to pick him up that night, even though she was supposed to. She knew that thinking in what ifs would make her crazy, but some days she couldn't help but wonder... if she'd been the one driving, if she'd been there to pick him up, would he still be alive?

She tried not to be bitter about it, though, and to appreciate Casey's kids for who they were. They were adorable... always bickering and getting into things, but adorable and extremely smart. Anna sighed at the memory of her baby boy, but knew that he was in a better place... no matter how much she wished he was still with her. It was like God made her heart sing with joy for a few years before deciding to repeatedly choke the life out of it with His bare hands.

Casey was 27, loud and crazy, but always fun and mostly reasonable. The loud part was what really struck Anna because she was such a quiet person herself. The crazy part was obvious as Casey had black and bright purple hair framing her slightly freckled face and complementing her vibrant green eyes.

Anna was in her mid-thirties and sometimes felt like they had nothing in common. Most times, though, their opinions matched up well and they felt comfortable talking about anything and everything. They also both worked from home and dealt with clients on a regular basis, which made for some interesting conversations. Every freelancer has clients from hell sometimes!

Anna loved the fact that Casey would randomly stop by and kidnap her for a night out, usually to drink pitchers of beer and sing karaoke at the tiny bar in town. Casey was a single mom, emphasis on *single* – she loved to go out and have a good time once in a while. Anna was usually home working, reading, or watching TV, and sometimes they even planned their excursions, usually no more than twice a month. Babysitters could get expensive for three kids, and Anna was kind of a hermit.

"So, any men in your life these days?" Casey asked with a glimmer in her green eyes. "You'd better not be holding out on me," she added with a huge grin.

"I have *no* prospects," Anna admitted with a sigh, her mind wandering to her online dating profile. She hadn't even bothered checking it for months... *that* was how interested she was in men at that point. She figured if it was meant to happen, it would happen. Casey knew her philosophy, of course, and immediately interjected.

"You're never going to meet anyone if you don't put yourself out there!" she exclaimed.

The waiter brought their food and Anna was grateful for the brief distraction.

"My heart's just not in it," she told Casey, looking at the beautiful sandwich and bowl of *au jus* in front of her. "My life is comfortable and happy just the way it is, so I don't really know that I want to put a conscious effort into attracting drama and craziness. Besides, most of the so-called men on these dating sites only message you for sex." Really, Anna just felt like she couldn't trust anyone. Her ex-husband had abandoned her when she needed him most, which made the entire prospect of dating seem self-damaging.

Casey cut a chunk off of her steak. She made sure she had some pepperoncini slices on the piece about to traverse to her stomach, then dipped it generously in steak sauce before shoving it in her mouth.

This was a woman who did *not* care what other people thought. She was never concerned with appearances unless in a professional setting, and she didn't pretend to be anyone she wasn't. Anna had been envious when they first met because she was so shy and *did* care what others thought of her. Anna's confidence just didn't soar quite like her friend's, especially since her skin started developing the weird sores she hid under layers of clothing.

"Maybe you need some motivation," she mused with a little smirk. "I could always text you the calendar boy pictures I get on my phone every day, ha! Would that help you get your heart in it?"

They both laughed. Anna wasn't interested in toned bodies or six-pack abs. She was more connection-oriented. Personalities and chemistry had to intertwine well for her, and faces were the most important part. She kind of had a thing about straight teeth, too, but that was secondary to at least *having* teeth! What really mattered was a good face, a compatible personality, and being able to have meaningful conversations, act goofy together, and be comfortable. Everything else was just superficial fluff for romance novels that had a snowball's chance in hell of ever being true. Casey knew this, too, and left it at that.

"Alright, well tell me what you're working on right now. Movie poster? Holiday card? Or are you doing what I *should* be and actually working on your own projects?" This question brought a huge smile to Anna's face.

"I just sold a piece," she stated with pride as she flipped her brown hair back behind her shoulder. "You know the little girl, Sophia, who I give art lessons to? Her father bought an original from me recently. He paid me $5,000 for it, so now I can say it's a limited edition and raise the price on the numbered prints."

"Congratulations!" Casey's blue eyes lit up. "That's amazing! I'm so proud of you," she added. "You're still open to doing my book covers, right?"

Anna laughed. "Nah, I'll just take this five grand and retire," she stated and both women chuckled. "I can't wait to do your book covers," she said in earnest. "You just need to let me know what I'm painting so that I can start! I can officially not worry about money for about two months before I start freaking out, so you can tell me now... or wait for next time," she added.

"I don't know yet!" Casey groaned. "I'm still writing and kind of looking for that scene that will inspire the cover. I think if you see it in your head and it feels right then that's the one, you know?" Anna nodded.

"How are the kiddos? I feel like I haven't seen them in a really long time. I bet they're huge!"

Casey let out a short laugh. "You wouldn't believe the things that come out of their mouths! They crack me up so much that I can't remember it all," she said. "Like the other day, Lisa told me very matter-of-factly that she didn't want to go to college. I asked her why and she told me there were too many crazy parties and she wouldn't be able to sleep."

Anna's eyes widened. "Wow, what in the world? And that begs the question... what are you letting them watch where there are college parties involved?" Casey's expression became serious.

"That's the thing... I have no idea where she's hearing this stuff. It kind of makes me wonder, you know? Then Jason decided to try to shave and cut himself with the razor. He was in the bathroom for *maybe* two minutes. The kicker? One of those cuts was *on his tongue*. Tell me how in the world trying to shave his tongue made any sense in his head? Six-year-old logic, right? I can't make this stuff up!"

Anna chuckled. "Well, they do say the most creative kids are also the most destructive," she offered. Casey just shrugged and smiled.

"They're definitely *my* kids," she stated, perfectly comfortable with her family's chaotic weirdness.

The friends enjoyed the rest of their meal together, knowing that they might not have a chance to do this again for a while. Anna loved the distraction. She hadn't been feeling quite right lately and Casey's company brought her back to a happier reality.

∞

Waking up in a cold sweat, Anna rolled over only to fall onto the living room floor with a thud. *The couch again,* she thought. *Wonderful.* Elbow throbbing from the impact, she made her way to the kitchen and turned on the light, groggy as she mechanically filled a glass with crushed ice and water from the fridge. She absently twirled her finger through her wavy brown hair and closed her hazel eyes as she took slow, deliberate sips.

It was always the same dream. She was just waking up, feeling woozy and disoriented. Above her was a bright white light, like in a hospital, and there were always two or more silhouettes standing over her, speaking in muffled and distorted tones. Then there was a feeling, like she was being tugged at... a pulling sensation, but she could never tell what part of her body was being tugged or why. She was just being yanked at and felt like the shadows wanted to take something from her.

Anna had been having these dreams ever since the ulcerous sores began showing up on her skin. When she looked up her symptoms online, she found a condition called Morgellons disease, but she wasn't sure what to do about it because it was apparently an incurable and mysterious condition. The sores produced tiny colored strings from time to time that she would pick at and pull until they came out from under her skin. She just figured they were fuzz left over from whatever she was wearing, stuck in the never-healing scabs that appeared out of nowhere on random parts of her body. She often felt itchy, like something was crawling around between the layers of her skin. She found herself feeling paranoid and having weird dreams, and she concluded that her dreams probably caused the paranoia.

Running through these facts in her head always made her feel vulnerable and somehow guilty, like she knew or had something she wasn't supposed to. It was the strangest thing she'd ever experienced. She'd always been reasonable, too. Nothing weird or crazy usually happened to her and she liked it that way. A drama-free existence. *Apparently not anymore,* she thought as she set her empty glass on the counter.

She wondered if maybe she was spending too much time alone, or maybe she was watching or listening to something that affected her subconscious and translated into the weird dreams. Maybe there was something she was too close to so she couldn't see it for what it was.

She dragged her feet as she made her way upstairs to her bedroom, the soft down comforter a welcoming sensation after her fall from the couch. *I need to stop falling asleep down there,* she thought as she drifted off to sleep, cocooned in her blanket so only her nose stuck out.

∞

As Anna walked home through the glistening streets of Deeplake, Washington, she adjusted her scarf and wrapped her coat around herself tightly, her breath fogging up the air in front of her. After a brief glance over her shoulder, she quickened her pace, her bag of groceries teetering in her arms momentarily as she adjusted her grip.

She'd been feeling like someone was watching or following her for weeks. At first she just shrugged it off as her own overactive imagination, but the other day, she could've sworn she saw a shadow out of the corner of her eye. When she looked, there was nothing there. That wasn't the first time she had seen shadows. They were always there, just out of sight, their existence never confirmed by a direct glance. But every time it happened, she got goosebumps and the hair on the back of her neck stood on end like it does when you know someone is watching you. It definitely didn't help that they reminded her of the silhouettes in her dreams.

Her left eye began to feel itchy and grainy as she walked, and she cursed herself for not driving. She blinked several times, but after a few moments her eye felt like it had sand in it again. This was accompanied by an unpleasant tickling sensation, which became annoying very quickly.

Her thoughts wandered as her eye got worse. She felt guilty but justified for not mentioning her problems to Casey, who had more than enough on her plate already. She also didn't want to come across as crazy; Anna was certain she wasn't. Some of the recent events in her life were crazy, but *she* was definitely sane.

Do crazy people think they're sane?

13

As she got to the front door of her split-level house, she fumbled for the keys with icy hands and unlocked the deadbolt. She closed the door as soon as she was inside, locking the deadbolt, the door knob, and the chain after a brief glance down her street in each direction.

She sighed as she took off her coat, her skin tingling obnoxiously. She shivered as the usual crawling sensation took over. *I wish that would just stop*, she thought. She rubbed her arm as she wandered into the kitchen, avoiding the sores that had begun developing on her skin several months before.

At first she had shrugged it off as accidental. Maybe she bumped herself while sleeping or caught the corner of some furniture. But these wounds were different. They took an incredibly long time to heal, if they healed at all, and they seemed to be spreading. She just hoped that she wasn't contagious. So far, she didn't know anyone else who was infected, so she assumed that she wasn't.

As she bent to look in the fridge, her eyes got foggy, feeling grainy like she had an eyelash caught in there. She blinked again, clearing the fog for only a moment before it came back.

Annoyed and hoping the knot forming in her chest wouldn't get worse, she closed the fridge and went to the bathroom to investigate what was in her eye.

Flipping the light on, she looked at her gaunt reflection and wondered briefly how she had gotten to look so... *old.* She'd lost weight and was happy about that, but as she saw herself in the mirror, she thought she just looked sickly.

She inched toward the mirror, hoping and praying that her eye wasn't infected. It was irritated and red because she had rubbed it, but other than that it seemed fine. So *why* was it so irritated? She felt the tickling sensation again. It almost felt like something was moving around in her tear duct.

Leaning forward against the counter, she put her face right in front of the mirror and looked intently at her hazel eyes, trying hard not to blink away the sensations as their intensity grew. As she watched, she thought she saw her lower eyelid twitch. *Am I going crazy after all?* She looked closer.

She noticed that her lower eyelid was tinted purple. *No wonder I look so sick,* she thought, concentrating on her eyes. There it was again! Movement. Like a twitch but more fluid and subtle. Her tear duct felt

14

like it was getting warm. She blinked it away, trying to stay focused.

The heat became more intense. She squinted, refusing to look away. But as her eye burned, it started watering and the pain increased. She tried to keep watching, but the pain got too intense.

Still trying not to look away, she blinked and rubbed her eye again, the pain subsiding just enough for her to catch a glimpse of something blue – was it really blue? – peeking out of her tear duct. The more irritated her eyes became, the less she was able to see. They were on fire! She turned on the cold water and ran her fingers underneath, then patted her eyes.

That helped, so she continued to watch, squinting intently.

It *was* blue. A tiny blue string.

She swore there was a second thing – she couldn't tell what it was – coming out of her eye. Red?

"What the fuck is going *on?*" she said out loud, her chest tightening with anxiety.

Whatever it was, it was definitely moving. It was small, so she had to lean in close and squint to make it out, but it was definitely *something*. She waited for a few moments and splashed more cold water on her eyes. Had she gotten string in her eyes from her scarf or sweater? And if that was the case, why did it feel like it was *inside* her tear duct, trying to come out? And why would it be *moving?*

She washed her hands with soap hurriedly and put her index finger to her eye, hoping she could pull out whatever was stuck in there. She was so focused that the pain took a back seat. Pressing firmly against the inner corner of her eye, she quickly tried to scoop out whatever it was with her nail and looked at her index finger immediately, expecting to see blue and red strings under her nail.

All she got was moisture.

She looked back in the mirror and saw that the strings were still there.

She climbed onto the bathroom counter so she could get the closest look possible and snatched her tweezers from a small cup of makeup utensils sitting in the corner. Her hands trembled as she rinsed off the tweezers, adrenaline rushing through her veins as the pain in her eyes vied for her attention. Kneeling on the counter with her face inches from the glass, she pulled down on her lower lid and moved the tweezers toward her eye, trying to be quick without injuring herself.

Wincing slightly, she grabbed the blue string with the tip of her tweezers and started pulling only to feel blinding white pain. She cried out and lost her balance slightly, but went right back to her task. She clenched her teeth and let out a whimper, not letting go of the miniscule blue string.

She pulled harder, letting out a groan as the burning sensation increased and pressure built up in her lower eyelid. It felt like she was giving birth out of her tear duct. Bracing herself with her other hand, she sucked in a deep breath, clenched her teeth, and pulled... hard.

∞

Anna woke up with a splitting headache. Blinking and trying to move, she looked around to find herself sprawled across the top of the toilet seat, her head against the wall at an awkward angle. Her neck ached and her brain felt like it would explode any second. Cold water still rushed into the sink.

She pushed herself up and looked behind her, mildly surprised to see that the wall was intact. She remembered intense, white-hot pain flooding her head through her eye and checked the counter for the tweezers, which had fortunately landed beside the edge of the sink, tip outward.

Standing slowly with her palm pressed to her eye, she spotted a tiny clump on the counter not far from the tweezers. It looked like balled up blue and red string wrapped in eye goo. But when she touched it gingerly with her fingertip, it felt hard, similar to rock or crystals. She turned off the water.

Not wanting to leave this cluster of strange unattended, she picked up the tweezers again and pinched the whole mess between the tips. Cupping her left hand underneath, she took it to a kitchen counter and turned on the overhead light.

Squinting her hazel eyes, she poked at the tiny mass with the tip of the tweezers, suddenly wishing she had another pair.

"What the hell *are* you...?" she muttered under her breath, trying to keep her breathing shallow so she wouldn't accidentally exhale it away and lose it. She noted that her eye felt perfectly fine. A little sore, but not bad. She decided to get a toothpick from the silverware drawer and pinched the balled up fibers in the tips of the tweezers again. Just in case.

As she loosened the tweezers and brought the toothpick closer to the tear duct excretion, she watched the blue string she had pulled on stretch itself slowly toward the wood.

"No way," she muttered, moving the wooden toothpick closer. She moved it left, then right... each time she moved it, the tiny string followed. She saw the red one poking out from the tangled mass, too, and she dropped the tweezers and the toothpick, stepping back and taking a deep breath as she cupped her hand over her mouth.

What is *that?*

Mystified, afraid, and eager to find out what was wrong with her eyes, she grabbed a small sealable plastic baggie and put the anomaly inside. She rolled the bag up and stuffed it in her purse, grabbed her car keys, and sped to the nearest hospital in hopes of finding some answers.

∞

"What can I help you with?" a nurse asked from behind the front desk in the center of the main lobby.

Anna spoke softly, choosing her words carefully. "Does this hospital have some kind of research department or testing lab?" she asked.

The blonde nurse furrowed her perfectly shaped eyebrows and nodded slowly. "Yea, it does... we usually don't let people back there, though. Can I help you with something?"

I doubt it, Anna thought wryly. Pursing her full lips, she took the sandwich bag out of her oversized purse.

"Maybe. I really need to know what this is."

The nurse snatched the bag from Anna, who almost snapped at her for it. She took a deep, calming breath and said nothing as the rude nurse examined the bag's contents.

"Well, it looks like a little ball of string," she stated. Her eyes spoke volumes of judgment and criticism as she handed the bag back to Anna, who promptly shoved it deep into her denim pocket.

"I pulled that out of my *tear duct* tonight," Anna whispered, hoping the urgency was communicated.

The nurse's reaction was minimal, though her eyebrows were raised in condescending skepticism. "What?"

"I'm sure you heard me," Anna replied, beginning to feel irritation building up. "I need to know what this is, *exactly*, and the only people who can tell me that are in the lab."

The nurse shook her head slightly, as if in pity. She looked behind Anna, left then right, and smiled as she focused back on Anna.

"I'm sorry, but I still can't just let you go in there," she said evenly.

Anna felt hands land on both of her shoulders as two men on either side of her began to steer her toward an elevator. Anna stepped out of their grasp and took a few paces backwards. The uniformed men turned slightly to look at her.

"What do you think you're doing?" she asked, crossing her arms and taking a solid stance.

"Ma'am, if you want to go to the lab, we'll have to escort you." The one on the right towered over her 5'7" frame at about 6'2", while the one on the left was only a couple of inches taller than she was and stocky.

Anna relaxed a little. "Don't touch me," she said finally and walked back toward the men, who both raised their hands in a gesture of surrender and stepped away from her.

Reluctant and wary with a sinking feeling in her stomach, Anna stepped onto the elevator in hopes that they would keep their hands to themselves.

The trio stood, uncomfortably waiting for the doors to close. Once they did, Anna felt tension fill the air. Before she could react, the men grabbed her and jabbed a needle into her neck. She went limp.

Chapter Two

Anna watched sleepily through her dark eyelashes as the nurses worked, wondering what they would find out. She was no longer afraid or nervous about it. Though she was aware that she wasn't completely safe, she simply hoped that they would figure out what was wrong with her eyes and her skin. Music played in her head and she closed her eyes again, sinking into a dreamless sleep.

∞

"Well, there's not much we can do," a voice made its way through Anna's veil of sleep.

"What do you mean? We can hold her for 72 hours. *Shh,*" another voice said, and both went silent. Anna sighed deeply, half-tempted to open her eyes, but she really wanted to stay asleep. She felt like she was waking up in the middle of the night and definitely wasn't prepared to function.

So she rolled over and went back to sleep as a door clicked shut.

∞

Anna stretched as she woke, light streaming into a window to her left and illuminating unfamiliar surroundings. Her eyes shot open and she sat up, the sudden movement making her head ache as dizziness washed over her. She found herself in a sterile room with light green walls and sparse furniture. She lay in a hospital bed.

"Shit," she muttered. *Should've seen this one coming,* she thought cynically. *Note to self: don't expect anyone to actually help you. If you think your problem is crazy, chances are the hospital will, too!*

Anna let out a sigh and plopped back in the bed. She idly wondered if they locked the doors or not. It looked like a normal enough room. Maybe they didn't lock patients in. She'd never been in a psychiatric ward.

She got up and went to the door to see if it would open. Sure enough, it clicked open easily. She smiled.

Peeking out into the hall, Anna watched as a few people walked by her. Two of them were nurses, one blonde and another with dark hair. They both smiled at her. The others looked off. One girl walked by with her head down, looking through a curtain of greasy blonde hair at the floor immediately in front of her. She didn't seem to notice Anna.

Another girl walked by, no older than 22, and she muttered something about a little boy holding a rose over and over.

Anna stepped out into the hallway from her room, taking care to remember her room number: 513.

Turning toward the nurse's station, she walked at a normal pace, taking in everything around her. Some of the room doors were left wide open, while others were cracked with curious, demented eyes staring out. Anna didn't feel like she was in danger from the patients, though. She was more skeptical of the staff.

"Excuse me," she said as she arrived at the station. No one even looked up. There were two female nurses working busily behind the partition. Anna cleared her throat loudly.

"Excuse me," she said more forcefully. That got their attention. The dark-skinned nurse walked over to where she stood and just looked at her with tired golden brown eyes, waiting for her to say something.

Anna offered a nervous half-smile. "I was wondering if I could speak to a doctor about why I'm here," Anna said.

The nurse just looked at her at first until she realized that Anna really *didn't* know why she was there.

"What's your name?" the nurse asked blandly from her seat.

"Anna Reynolds."

"Alright," the nurse said, clicking the computer mouse and scanning the screen. "It says here that you potentially have a condition we need to monitor and you'll be seeing a doctor tomorrow morning." The nurse looked up at Anna, still expressionless.

"Tomorrow? I have to get home before then," Anna said, starting to feel the familiar knot forming in her chest.

"I'm afraid we're holding you for 72 hours to monitor your condition," the nurse said mechanically.

Anna's eyes grew wide as she realized how long 72 hours was. "What am I supposed to do about work? I have clients who depend on me," she stated, a hint of panic in her voice.

The nurse looked at her wearily. "Your clients will just have to wait, Ms. Reynolds. That's all I can tell you right now." With that, she looked at the monitor and proceeded to ignore Anna, who turned around and stalked back to her room.

Once there, she wasn't sure what to do with herself. She lay down on the bed and listened to the whirring of fluorescent lights, steady background noise accompanied by muffled scuffling, conversations, and the occasional yelling match beyond her door. Though she was feeling a little tired, she knew that sleeping during the day would only make her restless at night.

She was bored out of her mind within thirty minutes.

If people aren't already crazy when they get here, they sure as hell will be after being here for a while, she joked with herself.

Her door opened with a *click* and one of the nurses poked her head in.

"Anna Reynolds?" she said. Anna nodded. "It's time for group therapy. Follow me." The nurse seemed friendly enough, so Anna got up from where she lay and followed the petite brunette woman in pastel pink scrubs down the hall to a larger room where a number of patients were gathered in a circle, all sitting in folding chairs. There was an empty chair for Anna and another empty chair for the doctor, who had chosen to stand. She immediately noticed the faint scent of too many people in one room, a stuffy blend of body odor and greasy hair. She tried not to make a face.

It was easy for Anna to distinguish the doctor as she saw the other patients. Some of them looked like they were just there to sleep, while others had strange looks in their eyes and scratched or picked at their skin or sleeves. Most had messy hair, some short and some long, and they all wore very basic clothing. She wasn't sure what to make of any of it, but then again she'd never been deemed potentially insane before. She slouched in her chair and sighed, waiting for the doctor to start talking.

He turned around and smiled as he looked at his patients.

"Hello, everyone!" he said cheerfully.

"Hello, Dr. Mitchell," the room replied. Anna slouched more, wishing she were invisible.

"Who do we have today that's new?" the doctor asked. "Let's see some hands."

Anna halfheartedly raised her left hand, dreading what singling herself out might provoke. Was this like prison movies? Or was a psych ward another beast entirely?

"Alright, we've got one new face with us today. What's your name, miss?" Anna lowered her hand.

"My name is Anna," she replied softly. *And I shouldn't be here,* her thoughts grumbled as if she were forced to attend some deranged AA meeting.

"Welcome, Anna," Dr. Mitchell said with a warm smile, flashing his straight, white teeth. "I hope you'll participate with us today, but I won't require you to until tomorrow. Sound fair?"

Anna nodded and let out a tiny sigh of relief, hoping that no one would bother her. The doctor pushed up his glasses and took a seat in his chair. He seemed pretty young, but Anna couldn't tell for sure as he leaned forward and rested his elbows on his knees while clasping his hands loosely.

She zoned out for a while, staring out the window at a lone evergreen tree. They had made her put on hospital clothes, which she hated because the sleeves were too short to hide her wounds. She couldn't believe that they just stuck her in here with no explanation.

"Anna?" the doctor said warmly. Anna jolted back to reality and gave him a deer-in-headlights look.

"Yes?" she said, looking around. Everyone was gone. Dr. Mitchell looked down at her and offered his hand to help her stand up. The sleeves of his pale blue button-up shirt were partially rolled up and she noticed that he wore a gold and black watch.

"I think you dozed off there," he said with a slight laugh. "Are you okay?"

She took his warm hand and let him help her up, wondering how that had happened. Sudden lapses in consciousness? Maybe she *was* supposed to be here. She had a bewildered look on her face and realized it when the doctor stopped smiling.

"Anna... are you okay?" he asked again, concern veiling his usual cheerfulness.

"I—I don't know," she replied, gingerly opting for honesty. "I didn't even know I fell asleep." She looked down at her hands, picking at a hangnail. Dr. Mitchell put his hand on her shoulder and gently led her to a plain desk at the front of the room. There were two chairs there, one behind the desk and one facing it. He motioned for her to sit down.

"Have a seat for a few minutes, okay?" he said with concern in his voice. "I understand you were just admitted, not of your own volition?" Anna nodded. She observed his face and noticed how sincere his gentle brown eyes were. When she'd gotten there, she thought he was a little too chipper.

"The front desk clerk," Anna began, "she just looked at the guards and they grabbed me. All I needed was a lab or some kind of testing done so I could figure out what keeps coming out of my body." The doctor furrowed his thick eyebrows and absently tugged at his goatee.

"What do you mean, coming out of your body? Can you describe that for me?"

Anna sighed. She didn't know if she should be talking about this with anyone now, especially a doctor. He would just confirm that she was crazy. But she felt enough of a combination of trust and doubt that she decided to open up after several moments of pulling on her earlobe in deliberation.

"Alright," she said. "But you'll probably think I'm crazy, just like all these other people in here." Dr. Mitchell chuckled.

"Honestly, I don't think anyone in here is *crazy*," he replied. Anna raised her eyebrows. He let out another short laugh. "I think that people deal with emotional hardships and trauma very differently. Those who deal with things too differently for others' comfort are sent here because they make so-called normal people uneasy." He air-quoted the word 'normal' and then crossed his arms and leaned back in his chair. Anna was a little surprised.

"But aren't you... a doctor? I thought your job was to diagnose people." He uncrossed his arms and sat forward again, resting his elbows on the desk and loosely clasping his hands.

"Well, yea," he began. "But my job is also to *help* people, and no one's helping anyone by calling them crazy or judging them." He said this with a conviction that made Anna's stomach flutter. Could he be someone who might understand? *Help*, even?

Anna nodded her head slowly. "Okay," she said, visibly relaxing. "I think I understand," she added.

"Good," he said, the beaming smile returning to his face. "Anna, why did they admit you?" he asked, genuine interest and curiosity in his brown eyes.

"My eyes were bothering me when I was walking home," she began. "So when I got there, I went to the bathroom to see why my eyes were so irritated. I thought that maybe I had an eyelash in my eye or something. Pinkeye. Whatever." She paused and took a breath, looking down for a moment. "When I looked in the mirror, my lower left eyelid was purple, like I hadn't slept in a week. It was also tickling or twitching or something, so I leaned in to get a closer look." She paused again and looked up at the doctor, who was studying her as she told her story. "There was a weird string-looking thing in the corner of my eye. It was blue. At that point my eye felt like it was on fire. Then I saw another string and it was red, next to the blue one."

"What did you do?" Dr. Mitchell asked. He was somewhere between morbid curiosity and concern, but Anna wasn't sure. She had told enough of the story for him to think she was a weirdo already, so she launched into the rest hurriedly.

"I tried to get it with my fingers and it didn't want to move. So I got some tweezers and started pulling, which was agonizing. I splashed my eyes with cold water, braced myself, grabbed the weird string, and yanked as hard as I could." Dr. Mitchell raised his eyebrows.

"It was painful?"

"Of course it was painful," she replied. "I woke up some time later sprawled across the toilet. I was lucky I didn't injure myself," she realized out loud, nervously twirling her brown hair around her finger.

"That you were," the doctor agreed. "And was that when you came here to see if someone would test the thing you pulled from your eye?" Anna nodded.

"Yep... and now look at me. In a psych ward talking to a shrink." Dr. Mitchell touched her hand and she looked up.

"Where is it now?" he asked, lowering his voice. Anna furrowed her brows at him.

"What?" she whispered.

"The thing you pulled from your eye," he replied. She narrowed her hazel eyes at him, wondering what he was getting at and why he was suddenly so hush-hush about it.

"Why?" she asked.

"Well... you're here, in a building with a laboratory." A sly smile tugged at one corner of his mouth.

"Are you suggesting—"

"Of course not," the doctor cut her off. "But I do want to help you, and I've never seen this before," he said. "If what you're saying is true, then it's my duty to find out what it is that's causing this." He gestured toward the blotchy, misshapen wounds on her arms.

"So you'll help me?" she asked. Dr. Mitchell smiled.

"Yes, Anna. I'll help you."

"How?" she asked.

"Where was the last place you had the specimen?" he asked. He stood, so Anna stood, too.

"In a zippered baggie in my jeans pocket," she said. He started toward the door.

"Alright. I don't have anything going on up here for at least an hour," he began, sounding eager. "I'll get it and take it down to the lab for testing."

"What will you say it's for?"

"I'm not sure yet, but I have a friend in the lab. We're going to figure out what this is."

Anna smiled and thanked him as he walked out of the room. She stood there for a moment, unsure of what to make of the situation. On one hand she was glad that he was helping, but on the other hand... well, she didn't know what was on the other hand, but it made her feel conflicted and she had no idea why.

She sighed and made her way back to her room, thinking about home and Casey. Anna didn't even have her cell phone on her because they confiscated it when they admitted her.

When she got back to her room she crawled into bed, letting her eyelids close and focusing on the sound of the lights overhead, trying to clear her mind and relax. She was just sliding into hypnagogia when a distant but familiar voice broke through the monotonous whirr of the lights overhead.

"You can't keep her here!" Casey shouted.

"Ma'am, you can't come in here without signing in," a nurse said sternly.

"I don't care! Did she check herself in? No? Well, then why is she here?"

Anna's door opened and slammed almost immediately after that. She hadn't even bothered to sit up on the bed as she opened her eyes. She knew she was trapped for a few days.

"Anna!" Casey said, relieved. "You're okay! I was so worried when you didn't answer your phone, I thought something horrible happened!" Casey sat down on the edge of Anna's bed and took one of her hands.

"Nothing terrible happened. It's just something that's been

going on for a few months and I finally tried to get it checked out...."
She hesitated at Casey's puzzled expression and knew she'd have to tell
her about her mystery condition.

"I started feeling all itchy and like my skin was crawling a while
ago," she began. "Then I started getting these random open sores all
over the place that won't heal and little strings keep coming out of
them. I pulled a clump of those same strings out of my tear duct and
came here to try to have it analyzed. Before I knew what was happening,
they detained me. They sedated me and everything." Casey's green eyes
widened.

"Can they even legally *do* that?" she asked in disbelief.

"I didn't think so, but apparently they can."

"Well, are they at least doing something to help you?" she asked.
Anna sat up and put her index finger to her lips.

"One of the doctors took the sample down to the lab to be
tested," Anna told her quietly. "I don't think anyone knows and I know
he didn't get permission, so don't say anything." Casey had a weird
smile on her face.

"You've been here for a day and already have a doctor flirting
with you?" she teased. Anna blushed.

"Of course not! I fell asleep in group therapy this morning and
he woke me up. He seemed really concerned so I told him what
happened." Casey smiled.

"Whatever you say," she said. "But I bet he's hot," she added.
Anna hadn't even thought about it.

"You know," she considered, "he's attractive in a very proper
kind of way. But I wouldn't call him hot, he's more... handsome. Like
a prince with a goatee," Anna added and they both giggled.

Casey stayed for an hour and the two talked. Anna had already
told the staff that she hadn't signed herself in so she wasn't paying for
anything. She'd also mentioned that they should be grateful if she
didn't sue the hospital for the stunt they pulled to admit her. Anna
honestly wasn't sure if they could even keep her legally, but she let it
go. There was no use arguing with people who thought she was crazy.

∞

Anna's mind drifted as she tried to fall asleep that night. She was
acutely aware of her crawling skin and its various open sores. She felt

itchy all over. Between that and her brain refusing to shut up, she wasn't sure how long she'd be awake.

She must've laid there for a good hour before she got up and started pacing. She wondered if they would give her some sleeping pills so she could just pass out. Her forearms itched and she rubbed them delicately, careful not to hurt herself more.

As she ran her hand down her arm, her fingers caught on something. There was a new clump of fibers protruding, and it felt like there was some kind of lump underneath her skin.

"Great," she mumbled. Looking at her arm in the dim light coming from the window, she started pulling gently at the fibers, hoping to pull at least some of the mess out of her arm. They were still pretty stuck. She would have to wait until her body pushed them out more.

She sighed as she sat down on the bed, a weird feeling of being watched washing over her. The room was dark, so she couldn't be sure of anything. Shadows always played weird tricks on her, especially after she'd started seeing moving ones, and she'd asked herself a million times if she was perceiving them more often simply because she thought she'd seen them before. It was a vicious cycle.

Unsure of what else to do, she lay back on her bed and closed her eyes, focusing on her breathing. The feeling of being watched grew stronger as she tried to relax, and a knot began to form in her stomach. The bridge of her nose tickled the way it does when someone is really close but not quite touching it.

She opened her eyes quickly and saw a black shadowy silhouette floating just inches above her. Her eyes widened and she stayed quiet, but fear gripped her with its icy fingers and she felt paralyzed as her breathing became ragged. The shadow above her looked like a face, but not entirely human. Its eyes glowed a dim red and it was staring directly into her eyes. She couldn't make out any distinct facial features, so she focused on her breathing... and not having a heart attack.

After what seemed like an eternity of being unable to move, Anna squeezed her eyes shut and mumbled, "You're not real, you're not real, you're not real...."

She opened her eyes and there was nothing there.

∞

27

Anna woke up in a daze, feeling groggy. As her eyes opened, she saw Dr. Mitchell looking at her with a soft expression from his seat next to her bed.

"How are you feeling, Anna?" he asked. She groaned and tried to sit up, but ended up laying back down. "I feel weak. What did they give me?" she asked.

"Just a mild sedative," he answered. "Don't worry; you'll be back to normal in no time. You were very distraught last night." The doctor smiled at her gently as she felt her eyelids flutter.

∞

"This is remarkable, though," a voice broke through the darkness of Anna's slumber.

"How is it remarkable? It's just one more nut case trying to get attention." The second voice sounded irritated and stressed out.

"That's why I feel like we need to run more tests," the first voice said. "There cannot be thousands of unrelated cases involving people who simply go crazy and then end up with the same exact symptoms."

"Why not? People go nuts all the time," the second voice retorted.

"But normally a mass hallucination or disorder is linked somehow... location, another disorder, a disease that would show up during testing... something. None of these cases have been related and they're all so similar."

Anna stirred and opened her eyes, ready to find out what both of these doctors had to tell her.

"So, what's wrong with me?" she asked them sleepily, propping herself up on her elbows in her disheveled hospital bed.

They both sighed and walked over to her bedside, so she sat up. She stretched and let out a big yawn as they prepared their respective spiels about her condition.

"Well," the skeptic began, "we've only seen about twenty thousand cases with these sets of symptoms show up *nationally* since 2002," he stated. "That means whatever you have is rare."

"It's also mysterious," the enthusiastic doctor said. "No one is sure yet what's causing this or where it comes from, so there's a lot of speculation. People are calling it Morgellons disease." *I was right,* she thought.

"The good news," added the first doctor, "is that there's nothing physically wrong with you that we can tell right now. What kind of symptoms are you having besides the sores?"

Anna was quiet for a moment. "Well," she began, nervous about sharing too much, "I've been feeling like my skin is crawling... and have had an increase in anxiety over the past few weeks especially," she told the doctors. "I've also been feeling foggy, like my memories are just out of reach. Other than that, my muscles feel a little tired but I attribute that to not being 21 anymore." She smiled, opting not to tell them about the ominous shadows and nightmares.

"Have you been scratching your skin?"

Anna shook her head. "I use lotions and anti-itch cream regularly; that helps to keep me from scratching," she said. "When I do feel a need to scratch, I rub carefully instead so I don't hurt myself."

"Alright, Anna," the first doctor's blue eyes softened. "My name is Dr. Rogers, and this is Dr. Peterson," he said, and Anna shook hands with both of them.

"Let me ask you this," he went on. "When the sores begin to form, how does that feel?"

Anna frowned. "Like something is trying to break through my skin really slowly," she stated. The doctors exchanged a look.

"Alright, Anna," Dr. Rogers said. "Here's what we know and what your options are at this point." Anna leaned back and listened.

"Morgellons isn't fatal, so you don't have to worry about this disease killing you. The most common symptoms are the crawling skin feeling, open sores, and colored fibers that appear inside the sores and eventually come out. Other symptoms are short-term memory loss, fatigue, and difficulty concentrating." Anna's eyes widened. That definitely sounded crazy when someone said it out loud.

"But what causes it?" she asked.

"That's where everyone is having trouble. The people this is affecting are otherwise completely healthy people, save for some history and inclination toward mental illness and-or addiction. Though some of them have a history of mental illness, I still don't find it surprising that the issue is so controversial." Dr. Rogers was calm and professional as he spoke.

"Okay," she replied. "So what are my options?" she added.

"You can do one of two things," the doctor said. "You can stay here for more testing just to make sure, or you can go home and get an occasional checkup because we've already tested others and found absolutely nothing out of the ordinary except for their symptoms. The most common misdiagnosis is delusional parasitosis, which is why you were detained in the psych ward for testing."

Anna lowered her head and stared at her hands for a moment. After a considerable pause, she said, "Okay. I'll go home and get checked periodically."

"Alright. I'll draw up the paperwork." Dr. Rogers walked away, but Dr. Peterson hesitated in the doorway. He walked back to Anna's bed and asked to sit with her for a moment. She just nodded and gestured for him to have a seat.

"Anna, this a disorder that I've got an extremely active... *personal* interest in," he confided. "Because it's such a mystery and no one can explain it, I'm hoping to make progress on what causes this and how we can cure it."

"What are you saying?" Anna asked, intently focused on his face. He was an attractive man, which made it more difficult for her to concentrate on his actual words.

"I'd like you to consider staying for a few days," he said. "I could be the doctor who treats you; I've been researching and studying this disease since it first caught my attention in 2004 and would like to explore all of the options I can."

"Um... okay," Anna replied. "What about missing work and my financial situation? I mean, I can't afford to be here long-term, both because of time and money."

"You're right, that could be an issue when occupying a room." He paused, thinking. "I could treat you at your house if you wouldn't mind... come by after work free of charge. Would you be okay with that?"

Anna's eyes grew wide and she smiled. "Really?" she asked.

"Sure," Dr. Peterson said. "I'm taking a personal interest in this disease, so it would only be fair."

"Okay," she replied. "And I won't have to pay for anything?"

The doctor shook his head. "Nope," he stated with a smile. "I would just come by to check on you a couple of times a week, draw blood or take samples for further testing, and we'll try to figure out what's really going on."

Just then, Dr. Rogers returned with Anna's discharge papers.

"All set?" he asked. Anna nodded and took the small stack of paperwork to fill out.

∞

"It's good to be home," Anna mumbled with a relieved sigh. Her paranoia had subsided almost completely and the doctor had written her a prescription for the itching, the pain, and a topical ointment to help the sores heal... at least they hoped that was what would happen.

Anna was grateful that she'd stumbled upon a doctor who would explore this instead of just telling her she was crazy. She'd almost started *feeling* crazy when they detained her at the hospital.

As soon as she entered her house, she went for her laptop in the living room.

Morgellons, she typed into the search bar quickly, hoping to get more information from the internet this time. The results loaded and she began browsing through various websites and support groups, looking for anything that might indicate what was happening to her and where this disorder came from.

There were many mentions of delusional parasitosis, a psychological affliction that causes people to think they have bugs underneath their skin. An overwhelming number of people had been turned away by doctors who stated that their symptoms were psychosomatic.

Anna searched and read for a while before realizing how tired she was. She let out a yawn and looked at one of the sores on her forearm. It still looked moist and one of the fibers was protruding from it. Unsure of whether it would hurt or not, she started to pull at it.

The fiber loosened a little. It was dark blue and extremely small, difficult to grasp between her fingers. She got up to find some tweezers, but stopped short when the doorbell rang.

She spun around and went to answer the door, pleasantly surprised to see Dr. Peterson standing there.

"Well, hello, Doctor!" she exclaimed with a smile. He nodded his head politely.

"Good evening, Anna," he said, returning a warm smile.

"What can I do for you?" Anna asked, motioning for him to come in. "I wasn't expecting you for at least a couple of days."

"Well," he began, "I was in the neighborhood and wanted to stop by to see if you've found any more fibers in your wounds yet, since they probably didn't really care about that in the psych ward."

She couldn't help but chuckle at how bizarre that entire sentence sounded.

"As a matter of fact, I have." She pulled up her sleeve to show the doctor how her wounds were progressing.

"Do you mind if we get into some better light?" he asked. "I'd like to take a closer look."

Anna led him into the kitchen where she sat down and rested her arm on the table. She watched with curiosity as he examined her wounds, surprised that it didn't hurt as he carefully pulled and pushed on her skin. There was just more itching, and she couldn't decide whether she felt pain or annoyance.

"Do you mind if I try to take some of this out as a sample?" Dr. Peterson asked with a quick glance at Anna's face. She nodded.

"Go ahead," she said, intrigued to see what he might find and what the whole fiber would look like under a microscope. They hadn't let her see at the hospital.

Dr. Peterson smiled as he opened his bag and pulled out a case, unzipping it to reveal a number of small medical instruments.

After washing his hands at the kitchen sink, he snapped on a pair of rubber gloves and examined her further.

Curious but wanting to keep her mind off of blood and disease, she studied the doctor's face as he pored over her skin abnormalities intently. He was quite handsome, with dark brown hair and blue eyes. He had a compassionate face and full lips that revealed straight, white teeth when he smiled, one dimple magically appearing on his left cheek. She guessed that he was in his early forties.

"What's that?" she asked him suddenly, gesturing toward the supply kit with her head.

"That's for emergencies when a hospital isn't nearby," he replied. His voice was even and balanced, almost monotone as he spoke to her. *He's cute when he's concentrating,* she thought. Anna found it interesting that, no matter what you do best, you can still do it with some distractions around you. Apparently it was no different for a doctor.

"Do all doctors have these?" she asked.

"We're all supposed to. Not all doctors carry them around with them everywhere they go like I do, but that's a personal preference...." he trailed off.

Pausing for a few moments, he seemed especially intent on what he was doing. She was so enamored with watching him that she didn't feel a thing as he pulled out the fiber.

"Here we are," he said softly, holding up forceps with a long, dark blue fiber hanging from them. Anna smiled.

Working quickly with dexterous fingers, Dr. Peterson placed the fiber into a vial carefully before snapping on a lid.

"And there we have it," the doctor said. "Other than that, have you noticed anything else? Anything strange, maybe?" he questioned, taking off his gloves and throwing them into her kitchen trash can.

"Stranger than strings coming out of my body?" she asked. "No, not really. I mean, I've felt a little under the weather, but I figured that was just stress or a cold or something."

"Okay. I'm going to ask you about some specific symptoms," he began, scooting his chair a little closer to her and taking one of her hands in each of his.

Anna was acutely aware of his touch. She briefly wondered if that was acceptable for a doctor to do, but she dismissed it because she was enjoying it. Her worry still managed to break into her thoughts, though. *I don't need any more bad news,* she thought as her face visibly fell into a less cheerful expression.

"Have you felt overly tired or exhausted?" he asked. She nodded. "Okay. What about your skin... can you describe the sensations you're having?"

"It feels like there are bugs crawling all over me but just *under* my skin... it's really annoying, actually."

Dr. Peterson smiled sympathetically.

"That's the most common symptom, along with the sores and the fibers," Dr. Peterson said. He was still smiling and their eyes met for a moment before they both looked away and cleared their throats.

Suddenly feeling awkward, Dr. Peterson stood up and began packing his medical bag.

"How's your ability to focus?" he asked, neatly placing his supplies back into the bag. He ventured another glance at her and she smiled.

"My focus is fine," she replied. "I'll let you know if that changes, though."

"Good," Dr. Peterson stated, returning her smile. "On that note," he stood, extending his hand to Anna, "I'd better get going. I'll give you a call next time I plan to drop by so I don't startle you," he added with a chuckle.

"No problem, Doctor," she said, shaking his hand. "I look forward to hearing what you discover about this illness."

She accompanied him to the front door.

"Please," he said as he stood in the doorway about to leave, "call me Andrew."

Chapter Three

Andrew caught himself muttering on the way back to his car, frustrated that he'd shown any kind of emotion toward the subject. She was so sweet, though, he almost felt like he couldn't help himself.

It's still unprofessional, he scolded himself. *Unprofessional and it won't help the cause.*

Driving back to his house a few miles away, he thought about Jody and how long he'd been covertly searching for more people with Morgellons. The BQS would be happy to know he'd finally found another one, although it was a bittersweet find for him. Jody was his fiancée and had passed away several years earlier, and though it wasn't directly caused by her disease, Morgellons did play a significant part in her death.

He pulled the car into his driveway.

Upon entering his house, he pressed play on the answering machine and listened as he took off his coat and set down his bag.

Beep!

"Hey, man! Where are you tonight? I was really hoping to see you out for drinks with us. Call me back." Andrew smiled despite his melancholy nostalgia moments before. Jake always managed to cheer him up no matter how foul a mood he was in, so he put his jacket back on and headed to the bar where he knew his friend would be.

∞

"There you are!" Jake shouted, getting up to greet Andrew and give him a friendly half-hug.

"Yea, sorry," Andrew said. "I almost forgot until I got your message at my house. I was seeing a patient so my cell was off."

"No problem, bro. Come on! Have a seat, grab a beer." Jake motioned for Andrew to sit down at a table where two of their acquaintances were also enjoying a beer and laughing about something.

"Jimmy, Derek," Andrew greeted them, shaking each man's hand as he sat down. They nodded in acknowledgement and continued their conversation, Jake sitting with Andrew.

"So who's this new patient?" Jake asked with genuine curiosity. Jake had been a friend for many years, and though he didn't work in the medical field, he always took an active interest in Andrew's cases and liked to hear about what he was learning.

Andrew held up his index finger for a moment as he took a long swig of beer. It was that initial *aahhh* feeling that seemed to make all of the day's stress melt away and allowed him to relax. *There's nothing like a cold beer after a long day,* he thought, setting his bottle down.

"Well," he began, turning his attention back to his friend. "Her name is Anna," Andrew began. Jake's expression immediately turned from interest to jest as he raised his dark eyebrows.

"*Anna,* huh?" he said jokingly. "What *about* Anna?"

Andrew punched his friend in the arm teasingly, already feeling better.

"Shut up, man," he said with a smile. "She's got Morgellons," he added.

Jake's smile faded. "Isn't that—"

"Yea, it is," Andrew cut him off.

Jake shook his head. "Why would you want to put yourself through that again?" he asked, his brown eyes sympathetic.

Andrew sighed and took another long swig of his beer. "I want to know what's behind it," he said after a pause, knowing he couldn't tell his friend the whole truth. "I also want to be able to move on, but I feel like I can't until I figure out exactly what this thing is."

"It still won't bring her back," Jake offered.

Andrew smiled at him, finished off his beer, and promptly ordered another one.

"I know it won't bring her back," Andrew said. "But it'll answer some questions and clarify whether she killed herself because of the disease or if there was something else going on."

"Whoa, whoa, whoa," Jake interjected. "I know her note was cryptic, but I thought we agreed to drop the conspiracy theories? You know that this disease has a tendency to go hand in hand with mental illness."

"I just can't get it out of my mind," Andrew replied, shaking his head and taking a drink as soon as his second beer arrived. "I *knew* her, Jake. She wasn't crazy."

Jake raised his hands in a gesture of surrender. "Alright, man," he said earnestly. "I support you no matter what, you know that. Just trying to look out for you."

Andrew smiled. "I know. I'll keep you posted," he added. "So, how are you and Tracy getting along these days?" he asked, changing the subject.

But in his mind, he was still there. He half-listened to Jake as he went on about his fiancée, who was 150% immersed in planning their wedding and driving Jake crazy with what he considered insignificant details. Andrew wondered vaguely how Jake could afford a wedding on a glorified security guard's salary, but the thought sped by quickly.

He knew that Jody's note was nothing to be dismissive about. There was a nagging feeling about that note and Morgellons that just wouldn't leave him alone and he had to figure out why. Even though he worked with the Bureau of Quantum Sciences, they wouldn't give him any details. He had been a lower-level operative, knowing just enough to be willing to collect specimens and hand them over. There was a sense of relief about getting back to collecting specimens now that he was higher up in the food chain. Maybe he would actually get some answers this time.

He absently ordered another beer and tried to focus on what Jake was saying, but he couldn't shake that irritating feeling as he recalled what her suicide note had said.

I can't take it anymore.
They have to find another subject.
The crawling is driving me mad!
Andrew... please forgive me.
Jody

∞

Andrew woke from his sleep with a start, gasping for air and soaked in cold sweat. Taking a moment to catch his breath and calm his racing heart, memories from a recurring dream flooded his mind.

It was eerie, like most dreams tended to be... flashes of images and emotions that he couldn't quite place but always left him feeling disturbed. The two images that recurred most often were the sight of Jody's wounds with protruding fibers and her suicide note.

He sat up in bed and stood, pulling a soft blue robe around himself and wandering into the kitchen for a glass of water. As he reached the bottom step, the phone rang and he jumped.

It's 4:00 AM, he thought as he made his way toward the kitchen. He answered it.

"Who's this?" he asked, his voice raspy from just waking up. He wandered through the kitchen and dug through the fridge absent-mindedly.

"I... I'm sorry to—to disturb you—"

The sound of Anna sobbing snapped Andrew to full consciousness.

"Anna?" he said softly. "Are you okay? What's wrong?"

"I—," she began, her words interrupted by sobs of... what was that? Fear?

"Take a deep breath, Anna," he said into the mouthpiece soothingly. "It's okay... just breathe." He could hear her taking deep breaths and exhaling slowly, trying to calm herself. "That's it. Okay," he continued, "now what's going on? What happened?"

Anna took several more deep breaths before she spoke again.

"I'm scared," she whispered softly into the phone. "I don't know what's going on," she added. "I... I don't have anyone else I can call who can help," she said, her wavering voice laced with embarrassment.

"It's okay, Anna," he said reassuringly, his intrigue with her growing. "You can call me. I mean it *is* four in the morning, but for some reason I was awake anyway. What happened?"

She took another deep breath. "I was sleeping," she began shakily. "I had these terrible dreams, they were so real...."

"What happened in the dreams?" Andrew asked softly. He began to wonder if he should go over there to keep her company for an hour or two, make sure that she wasn't being psychologically impacted by the disorder. *Unprofessional!* a little voice in his head yelled. Ignoring it, he made his way back up to his bedroom to find clothes, just in case.

"There were shadows...."

Andrew furrowed his brows as déjà vu punched him in the stomach. He had heard this before.

"I felt like they wanted something from me, like they were there to take something away, but not to help me... to help themselves.... I'm sorry... I shouldn't have called you...."

"No, no, no," Andrew interrupted her, trying to remain soothing. "I'm glad you called me," he said. "I want to help. What do you need? Do you want me to come over?" he blurted before he could stop himself.

There was a pause. "I don't want to be alone," she whispered softly. "I'm afraid."

"Okay. You sound like you need some company," he said, trying to sound positive. "I'll be there in a few minutes, okay?"

There was another pause followed by a whisper. "Okay."

∞

By the time she was able to tell him the full extent of her nightmare, he was quite disturbed. He'd gotten similar accounts from Jody while they were together, before things had gotten *really* strange. He thought it was interesting — from a doctor's perspective — that they both had dreams about shadowy figures wanting to take something from them. And they both worded it the exact same way: *take* something from them, not that the figures simply *wanted* something from them.... They wanted to *take* something from them. The question was what?

Another question was, were these shadowy figures a side-effect of Morgellons and could this side-effect be treated? He had no idea what was going on behind the scenes with BQS wanting fiber specimens, but it looked more and more like he should be trying to find out more from them, or conduct some of his own tests and research on the fibers, which he thought was a better idea.

Andrew sat with Anna for a long time, listening to her stories about how things had been getting more and more bizarre over the past few weeks. It had been several days since he collected the last sample, but her situation was never far from his thoughts. This disease was just too weird, and the surrounding circumstances made it even stranger.

He wasn't much for conspiracy theories and considered himself to be a fairly reasonable man, but since the BQS had approached him and everything remained secretive and classified with them, his suspicions had only grown. What were these people up to?

∞

Anna squinted against the bright light suddenly in her eyes. Was she still asleep? Dreaming? She was disoriented and felt like she wasn't in her own body.

As she struggled to open her eyes, she got a sense that something was wrong. She tried to open them but could only manage to peek out through her eyelashes at her surroundings. The bright light was interrupted only by three tall silhouettes, shadows that loomed over her. Slightly alarmed but feeling numb, she wondered if she had been in some sort of accident and landed in the hospital again.

She couldn't feel anything except for a pleasant haze... foggy. It wasn't warm or cold... it was just there, a fuzzy feeling of blurriness similar to being drunk or on pain killers. Her mind screamed while her body refused to cooperate.

She suddenly felt a sharp pulling sensation on her legs, then more on her arms. She couldn't cry out, but a tear slid down her cheek and pooled in her ear. She couldn't move. That was the end of the numb haze.

What's going on? she wondered, trying to focus on the fuzzy feeling instead of the pulling and dread. The sensations continued and she felt herself rising to consciousness slowly, her eyelids becoming lighter.

Moments later, she was fully awake in her empty bedroom. Anna dialed Dr. Peterson's number without knowing why. She thought about her dream as the phone rang and wondered how it could've been so lucid. It was as though she wasn't really in a dream but somewhere between dreaming and awake. Why she had immediately – no, *instinctively* – called Dr. Peterson was beyond her understanding.

He arrived shortly after their phone call and Anna opened the door with a cautious smile.

"Hello, Doctor," she said, beckoning him inside.

"Hello, Anna," he replied with a smile. As he took off his coat, he reminded her, "Please, call me Andrew."

Anna flushed slightly and turned away, walking toward the kitchen. "That's right, you had said that," she replied nonchalantly. *What is* wrong *with me?* she wondered. Her fear immediately dissipated and she was focused on how her heart fluttered instead of telling the doctor what happened.

"How are you feeling?" Andrew asked her as he made his way into the kitchen behind her. He graciously accepted a hot mug of chamomile tea and smiled as she gestured for him to sit across from her.

Adjusting herself on the bar stool at the island counter in her kitchen, Anna shrugged and lifted the cup to her mouth, blowing on it slightly to cool the tea.

"I'm fine, I guess," she stated after a small sip. "Aside from feeling freaked out, I mean. Then again, it really wasn't horrible; no pain, just a drunk-like numbness." She took another sip of her tea. "The shadows were there again," she added.

"Again?" Andrew replied, pulling out a small memo pad to take notes. He glanced up at her. "You've had similar dreams before, then. Do you mind if I write some of this down?" he asked. She simply shook her head no. "Thank you," he said with a smile. "It might help with my research."

"Okay," she said, watching him as he scribbled in his notepad. "There was something pretty weird that happened, though," she said when the scratching of his pen slowed.

His head snapped up quickly to look at her, eyebrows raised. "Oh?" He focused on her fully, his curiosity piqued.

"Well...." she began slowly, lifting up her left pajama pant leg slightly. "Look at this," she added. He got up from his stool and stepped toward her on the other side of the island to check her leg.

"I don't see anything," he said, looking up at her with furrowed brows. "What am I supposed to see here?"

"Yesterday there were sores there," she pointed to a smooth spot on her shin, "and there." The other part was closer to her knee.

As he processed that information, Andrew's eyebrows raised slightly, his blue eyes incredulous.

"That's not possible," he stated. "No one can heal that rapidly. Did you happen to take pictures?" he asked her.

She shook her head, frowning. "No, I had no idea they would just vanish. It's never happened before."

"Alright," he replied, biting his lower lip as he considered their options. "Would you mind working with me on a system where we get pictures or documentation of some sort of your sores and where they are? This is very strange. I'd like to get to the bottom of it."

Anna nodded in agreement. "I think that's a good way to go," she said. "It will at least help me to feel more at ease if I know for sure that it *isn't* happening... you know... just in case I'm not entirely sane anymore. I don't know how this affects the brain, especially long-term...." she trailed off.

"I don't think you're crazy, Anna," Andrew told her with a reassuring smile. "Worried and frightened maybe, but not insane."

Anna smiled and Andrew sat back down in the stool across the island from her. They both sipped their tea in silence, each wandering through their own thoughts. After several minutes and leisurely sips of chamomile, they looked up and began to speak at the same time, resulting in a shared laugh.

"Ladies first," Andrew said, still smiling.

"Well," Anna began, slowly contemplating her wording. "This might be a little forward, and I hope you don't take offense," she continued. She paused briefly to take another sip of tea.

Andrew raised his eyebrows and smiled, his heart skipping a beat. *Don't do this to yourself*, he thought, composing himself quickly.

"What is it, Anna?" he asked, hoping he still sounded professional but highly doubting it.

"Well... I feel like I already know you," she said. "I don't know if that makes any sense or not, but I feel like you're an old friend or something."

Andrew smiled at her, showing off his pearly whites. "It makes perfect sense," he said, taking one of her hands. "You and I met because you have a rare condition and I have an uncommon interest in that condition... not to mention experience with it. Makes sense to me," he added, retracting his hands and finishing off his tea.

Anna's expression faltered a little with the realization that they were mostly on the same page, just not completely. She held her smile, nodded, and replied, "You're right. That must be it."

With that, Andrew stood and put his hand on Anna's shoulder in a comforting gesture. Looking at her intently, he said, "Don't forget to write down your wounds every day, and take pictures as documentation. We need to know everything we can about this affliction. That can help us find a cure."

Anna nodded in agreement and walked back to the front door with him.

"Thanks for coming at such short notice... and such a weird time," she told him, looking down in embarrassment. "I know I sounded pretty out of it on the phone."

"Don't worry about that, Anna." He folded his coat over his arm. "You're a special case," he added. "If you need *anything*, just let me know. That was why I gave you my personal number, after all." He beamed at her again and opened the door, disappearing into the suburban dawn and leaving Anna alone with her cup of chamomile.

Chapter Four

Over the next several weeks, Anna tried desperately to cover her wounds while simultaneously attempting to heal them with various ointments and home remedies. She figured that if there was anything out there that would help alleviate the sores, she would find it. She scoured the internet for solutions but found nothing except more dead ends and other people searching for answers. She caught herself several times wishing the magical overnight healing nightmares would happen again, but she wasn't sure if she actually wanted that.

Though there were a number of websites with treatment recommendations and suggestions, she wasn't at ease with trying them all to see which ones worked. She decided to speak to Andrew to narrow down her options.

Once she had made up her mind to work with Andrew on finding a way to suppress and treat her wounds topically, she gave up her search online and focused on documenting everything and working. She couldn't shake the feeling that there was a lot left to be discovered about her illness as well as her nightmares. To compound it all even more, she hadn't fully faced anything that happened over the past several years and it just kept trying to surface no matter how badly she wanted to let go. Her pain was the thumping of a bass drum that had been turned down to a lower volume, but she could still feel the vibrations of it from the recesses of her soul. She desperately missed her son.

∞

"Anna!" Andrew said into the receiver excitedly. "I think I found something that might work to help heal your skin."

Anna's face lit up with a smile. "Really? What is it?" Her imagination animatedly ran off with the notion of no itching and smooth skin.

"You'll have to come in because it's a process," he began. "I think I can help your skin get back to normal, though." There was a pause.

"What? And come in to where? The hospital?" Anna asked.

"Well... it probably won't stop the crawling feeling or the

itching," he told her. "As far as coming in, when I say that I mean to the clinic where I work. I do the lab stuff at the hospital part-time, so that's not usually where I am."

"Oh, okay," she answered, slightly disappointed that she may or may not feel entirely better. Quickly cheering up, she added, "Oh, well... At least I won't look like a monster anymore."

Andrew laughed. "A monster?" he asked. "Are you kidding me? You're beautiful." As soon as the words escaped into the mouthpiece of the phone, he wished that he could snatch them back. *Idiot!* he scolded himself. *Unprofessional!*

Anna blushed furiously. "Well, thank you, Andrew," she replied, sounding calm and detached. "I appreciate that," she added.

"You're welcome," Andrew said with relief that he hoped she wouldn't hear through the phone.

"So when should I come in?" Anna asked after a brief pause. "I'd like to begin as soon as possible... I can't even tell you how self-conscious I've gotten since this whole thing started."

"I'll bet," Andrew replied sympathetically. "I can't imagine what it must be like. How's the day after tomorrow around 3:00 PM?" he asked.

Anna smiled. "Perfect!"

"Great. I'll see you then, Anna."

"See you then.... Bye!"

∞

Before Anna could do anything else about her illness, she had to give little Sophia Schwartz an art lesson that had been put off for a couple of weeks. She wasn't sure why Dr. Schwartz had hired her; he'd found her on one of the freelance websites she used and made an odd request: to give his daughter art lessons in her home. While Anna had tried to explain that she wasn't a teacher, he insisted and offered her an amount of money per month that she couldn't refuse.

From the very first time Sophia had come over, Anna fell in love with her. She was a brilliant child, highly creative, intuitive, and intelligent, even though she was only ten. So Anna planned each lesson for several hours the day before and made sure she focused on technique first, then allowed Sophia to express her own emotions during the last part of each lesson.

Because they had several hours together each time, which normally happened weekly, Anna and Sophia got to know each other pretty well. She was looking forward to this lesson as she hadn't seen Sophia in a while and missed their time together.

"Hi, Sophia!" Anna exclaimed and gave her a hug. Dr. Schwartz didn't like to come to the door, probably because he was a busy man. Anna wasn't sure what kind of doctor he was, but he hadn't even flinched about Anna having Morgellons when she told him, which meant he probably knew at least a little bit about the condition.

"Hi, Anna!" Sophia replied, excitedly taking her jacket off and picking up her portfolio from where she had set it when she came in. "I missed you so much," she stated as they made their way into Anna's studio. She'd converted one of the large upstairs bedrooms into a sunroom so that she could get the best light for most of the day.

"I missed you, too, honey!" Anna said with a bright smile. "How have you been doing?"

"Fine... I just do my best in school and try to make as many friends as I can," she said with a smile.

"How are your grades?"

"Fine. I'm good at everything," she stated matter-of-factly.

"It would seem that way, wouldn't it?" Anna replied with a chuckle. "Do you have any ideas about what you'd like to work on today?"

"I want to learn more about the salt and watercolor technique because that was so *awesome* last time! Can we do more of that today please?" The sparkle in Sophia's eyes made Anna smile.

"Of course! If that's what you want to work on, that is what we'll work on," Anna replied. "I haven't had much of a chance to plan anything for today, so I'm glad you have something in mind that you're so excited about."

"Yay!" Sophia said with a little hop. "I'll get the supplies ready!"

Anna and Sophia got to work preparing some space in the studio for both of them to paint. Anna enjoyed teaching Sophia, who was a very eager student. Because she was naturally talented and intelligent, she mastered everything in a relatively short amount of time. Her enthusiasm for learning didn't hurt, either.

Anna watched the little blonde-haired, blue-eyed girl get all of her supplies neatly lined up within easy reach, and she couldn't help but smile. This was a wonderful distraction from her disease and that whole situation. Anna stared out the windows for a little bit, her thoughts drifting toward finding a cure.

"How are you feeling, Anna?" Sophia asked as she finished setting up and noticed that Anna was staring off into space.

"I'm okay," Anna said, snapping out of it. "I've just been having some trouble with my sickness lately," she added. Sophia had asked about the sores on Anna's arms during her very first lesson, being blunt and forthcoming like only children tend to be.

"I'm sorry," Sophia said sincerely. "I hope you get better soon," she offered with a smile.

"I'm sure I will. But let's focus, okay? What should we paint today?"

"Well, we did flowers last time, but can we do fruit with this technique? I want to paint some fruit," she said excitedly.

"Why does that not surprise me?" Anna said with a laugh. "You really are a little fruit bat, aren't you?" Dr. Schwartz had told Anna when they'd first met that Sophia absolutely loved fruit. It didn't matter what kind of fruit; if there was fruit as opposed to another kind of snack, she would choose the fruit every time.

Sophia nodded vigorously. "It's my favorite!" she said.

Anna had a basket of artificial fruit that she specifically used as a prop for painting, so she got that out and set it on a small table in the center of the room between them. With that, they set to work, using watercolors to paint the fruit and sprinkling salt on the page to achieve the desired effect.

Anna put on some music as they worked, and they both got lost in their creative zones for a while.

"How does this look?" Sophia asked Anna. Anna stopped what she was doing and went around to see how Sophia's painting was going. Though it wasn't perfect, she could tell that this little girl was developing into quite a good artist.

"It looks fantastic!" she said, smiling. "You do need to make your lines a little cleaner, but you did a wonderful job. I can't believe how fast you're catching on!" Anna added, giving Sophia a little sideways squeeze.

"Can I paint something else now?" she asked. Her mood seemed to have shifted.

"Of course, honey. Are you okay?"

"Yea...." Sophia hesitated. "It's just... sometimes I have bad dreams and remember stuff that doesn't seem right," she said. "I had one of those dreams last night and just remembered it, and I want to paint something sad. Or mad. Or both." Sophia sighed.

"That's perfectly fine," Anna said, slightly concerned. "You can take some time and paint whatever you want, okay? Your dad won't be back for another two hours, which gives us plenty of time."

"Thanks, Anna," Sophia said. "It's a bad feeling so I want to get rid of it," she added.

"I understand," Anna replied. "Do you want to talk about it?"

Sophia shook her head. "I don't know how to explain it," she said. "It's pain... on the inside of my body. And everywhere, not just one place. And that sounds so weird!" she added.

"It does, but you know that I totally understand weird, too," Anna said with a comforting smile.

Sophia smiled but didn't say anything else about it. Instead, she painted a dark, moonlit lake with someone drowning in the middle of it.

∞

The next afternoon, Anna felt a little nervous as she walked into Andrew's clinic. She had no idea what to expect since the treatment he'd proposed was untested. She assumed everything he was using would be safe and have few side-effects, but then she reconsidered her evaluation of side-effects. *Everything has side-effects*, she thought, opening the glass door and entering the clinic.

She approached the desk and smiled at the cheerful older brunette woman sitting at it.

"You must be Anna," the woman said with a bright smile. Her name tag read Nina.

"I am... is Dr. Peterson here?"

Nina nodded. "He's expecting you," she said. She pointed to the doors on her left. "Just follow the hall until the end and his office will be on the right."

Anna pushed open double doors and followed the long hallway toward Andrew's office while wearing a huge, cheesy grin. The door was slightly ajar, so Anna paused nervously in front of it to knock.

"Come in!" came the immediate reply.

Anna opened the door and walked into his office. *Is it weird that*

I'm so excited to see him? she wondered. She shook her head and composed herself, keeping her smile at a polite level as opposed to the blinding neon sign she wore walking down the hall where no one could see.

"Hi, Doct—I mean, Andrew," Anna said softly as he turned to welcome her with his own smile. He motioned for her to sit down in one of the chairs in front of his desk while he finished fiddling in a cabinet behind his executive chair.

"Anna," he said warmly after standing up. "It's wonderful to see you looking so content!" he added, taking her outstretched hand in both of his own and smiling as he sat down.

"How has your day been?" she asked casually, wondering what treatment she was looking forward to.

"Alright, I suppose," he replied, opening her file. "Same thing, different day, you know?" He looked up and smiled at her again. "Yours?"

"Fine," she said plainly. "I'm nervous to find out what this treatment will be like, so I was pretty restless today." She let out a slight chuckle.

"Not surprising!" he replied. "Alright. I won't keep you in suspense, then. Could you change into this gown and sit down on the exam table for me? I'll be back in a few minutes."

Anna nodded and he left the room as she made her way to a small exam room attached to his office.

Changing into the gown was the easy part. The hard part was staying seated once she had. It felt like it took him ages to get back into his office, so she was left to her own devices: bored in a doctor's office. *Correction,* she thought, *bored in a* sexy *doctor's office.* Her cheeks flushed at her own thoughts.

She stood, holding the back of her gown closed with her left hand as she wandered over to his desk. She knew she shouldn't be snooping, but he was taking forever and she couldn't satisfy her curiosity any other way.

Feeling playful, she sat down in Andrew's leather executive chair. It was comfortable. She opened one of his desk drawers. Nothing exciting there... paper, pens, a pair of glasses. She opened another to find a neatly organized filing drawer. She was pushing it closed when something caught her eye. Jerking the drawer back out, she did a double take on what she thought she'd seen. Sure enough, there it was. One of the folders was labeled *Morgellons* and had two files inside. One was labeled *Jody* and the other *Anna*.

A loud laugh and Andrew's voice yelling a response to someone in the hall made her shut the drawer and scramble back to the exam table. She hoped that he hadn't heard the commotion.

"Well, here we are," Andrew said with a smile. He was carrying two syringes with labels on the sides.

"Shots?" she asked, slightly confused. "I thought for sure the treatment would be topical."

Andrew looked up at her from where he was working. "For the Morgellons, it will be," he stated. "But after reviewing your file, I noticed that you haven't had your flu shot this year and it's been 12 years since your last tetanus booster. Are you okay with taking care of those today?" Anna didn't know it, but this was his way of making sure he had a legitimate reason for her to be there, covering his tracks.

Anna nodded. "Of course," she said. "I didn't realize I needed them." She paused for a moment, musing at how cleverly he was avoiding the real treatment she'd come in for. "How long do you plan to stall before getting into the Morgellons treatment?" she asked with a nervous smile. "Is it that bad?"

Andrew's smile faded as he gave her the first shot. "It's not that it's *bad, per se*... but I really don't know if it will work and have never done an experimental treatment before." He placed a small bandage on the dot of blood forming on her upper arm, then moved to her other side. All the while, she was acutely aware of his touch and found herself thoroughly enjoying his proximity to her. "I guess I'm a little bit nervous, too," he added with a smile, seamlessly giving her the second shot and placing a small bandage on her other arm.

"Okay, so what is it?" she asked with an impatient smile. "Don't keep me in suspense here," she added.

"Okay, here's the deal. We're going to try each treatment we come up with for a period of six to eight weeks to see if it works or not. Since this is not an official treatment and hasn't been cleared, we have to stick with options that can be done at home, are not invasive, and won't be traced back to me if we decide to use products that aren't available over-the-counter. Okay?"

Anna nodded, slightly concerned about the under-the-table approach, but looking forward to some semblance of progress. She found herself surprised by his willingness to use methods that weren't by the book, but since there was no legitimate or official treatment for Morgellons yet, she had figured something like this might happen.

"Couldn't you have just made this recommendation over the phone or the next time you come to my house?" she wondered out loud.

"I suppose I could have. I wanted to make sure you're alright otherwise, though. The psych ward at the hospital isn't exactly notorious for doing a good job with the basics," he added.

"Oh," she said, feeling a little more comfortable. "I guess they only specialize in one thing, right?" she added with a smile. Andrew smiled back.

"Alright," he said. "The first thing I'm going to recommend to you is called diatomaceous earth. Make sure the label says food-grade. Here," he pulled a folded piece of white paper from his pocket. "This is a recipe for a paste that should help alleviate the itching as well as help the sores to heal. Put this on your skin after showering or bathing and before you go to bed. And whatever you do, don't accidentally breathe in the Diatomaceous Earth in its dry form – it could irritate your lungs due to high levels of silica content."

"Okay...." Anna took the piece of paper from him and looked it over. "What is it? Will it hurt?" she asked.

Andrew shook his head. "It shouldn't," he said. "And if it does, then stop using it and we'll find another treatment. It's a finely ground powder made from fossilized diatoms, which are a type of hard-shelled algae. I know it sounds weird, but food grade diatomaceous earth can be taken as a supplement when mixed into a drink, or it can be applied to your skin."

"Alright," Anna said. "Any particular reason you wanted me to change into a gown for this little consult?" she asked coyly.

"Of course," he said with a flirtatious smile. "Your last physical was two years ago, Anna. I'd like to make sure you're in good health aside from this Morgellons craziness."

Anna smiled back. "Alright, I suppose I can handle that."

∞

As Anna got home, she was floating on endorphins from seeing Andrew again. She couldn't explain why she liked him so much, but it was fantastic and distracting at the same time. She didn't even know if he felt the same way, but a part of her thought he might. After she got down from her cloud, she pushed him to the back of her mind and tried to focus on the matter at hand: her first treatment. She'd gone to the local organic food store to buy what she needed to create the paste he gave her the recipe for.

Anna couldn't wait to try the first treatment on her wounds that night. The physical had gone well; she was in perfect health other than the obvious. He did recommend taking a daily vitamin to make sure she was getting all of the nutrients she needed, so she'd also picked up a generic multivitamin.

She ran a bath and decided to use only plain water. To relax, she had a glass of wine with her. It had been a while since she'd taken a bath and actually enjoyed it, so she decided that it would be a night for relaxation intertwined with newfound hope. As the tub filled with water, she lit a scented candle and took a sip from her glass of wine.

Closing her eyes, she sank back into her oversized tub, covered her eyes with a damp washcloth, and lost herself in thought for a while. She gingerly felt her way along the edge of the tub until she touched the stem of her wine glass and took it, leaning forward to take a sip. Setting it back on the edge of the tub, she leaned back into the steamy water and sighed, consciously willing her muscles to relax. For the first time in weeks, she felt comfortable, hopeful, and alive with possibilities about her illness... and about Andrew.

Chapter Five

"Did you get them?" a voice asked from the darkness across the dimly lit warehouse.

"Of course I did. What do you take me for?" Andrew was slightly offended at the question, but understood the need for caution. The BQS could be ruthless beyond imagination if things didn't go smoothly.

"Good. Show me so that I know they're not compromised. You know what the clients would do if the samples were damaged."

"Don't remind me...." Shuddering at the thought, he set a metal briefcase down on the long table in front of him. He snapped open the latches on either side to reveal the contents and stepped back from the table so his colleague could examine the fiber samples.

They kept this on a strictly confidential basis, so one was not allowed to see the other... at least not closely enough to make a positive identification under any circumstance, legal or otherwise. They both wore ski masks, which made Andrew feel way too much like a criminal cliché, but orders were orders.

Andrew turned his back to the table after backing away about ten feet, knowing that the lighting was too dim to pose a real threat. As he waited, he silently kicked himself for getting involved with these people in the first place. *Desperate times,* he thought wryly.

His associate took one of the vials out of the briefcase to study it. He opened the vial and took a fiber out with the tip of a pair of sterilized forceps as he shone a small light on it to make sure it was viable.

"Everything is in order," a voice said behind him. He stayed put and waited for payment to be placed on the table. After disappearing for about a minute, his associate returned with the usual: an envelope that he knew was full of crisp $100 bills. Removing the metal briefcase from the table, he replaced it with the envelope.

"A pleasure doing business with you, as always," he said.

Andrew took the envelope silently and left the warehouse, satisfied with its thickness. Walking out into the night, he breathed deeply, capturing an invigorating taste of the chilly air. A twinge of guilt tugged at his heart as Jody and then Anna crossed his mind, but he had to shake it off. According to the BQS, this was for the greater good, and he had to believe that to a certain degree to maintain his justifications for selling the Morgellons samples. He may have gotten into it with good intentions, but he knew he couldn't realistically get out... not without being hunted down for interrogation... or worse.

Before he knew what was happening, a darkly clothed man approached him stealthily from behind and plunged a syringe into the side of his neck. As consciousness was replaced by blackness, Andrew's body went limp and his attacker lowered him gently to the ground before dragging him to a nearby black car with darkly tinted windows and maneuvered him into the trunk.

∞

Anna woke with a start as her alarm went off. She'd had a hard time falling asleep and an even harder time staying that way because she was so nervous about how her first treatment would end up looking in the morning. Not that she expected much... Andrew had warned her not to get her hopes up because it would likely take at least two to four weeks for any real results to show, even if her wounds began to look like they were healing after a few days.

She got up, slipped into her robe, and made her way to the kitchen to brew a pot of coffee. On her way, she gingerly touched her skin where she knew some of the wounds were and winced as her fingernail caught a scab. She immediately felt disappointed, but dutifully reminded herself that this wasn't a miracle treatment and it might not even work.

Letting out a sigh and closing her eyes, she tried not to think about it too much and poured herself a cup of hot coffee.

Her laptop was on the island in the kitchen as it usually was. She smiled as she took her typical seat and opened the computer, looking forward to checking her email and seeing what the world was up to. She thought about doing more research on Morgellons, but she decided against it in favor of a morning session of Solitaire.

She lost herself in the computer card game and the bittersweet flavor of her cup of coffee. The truth was that she really didn't want to face any form of reality that day... nor had she for a number of days before, for that matter. Reality was just too much for her to handle lately. It seemed better to just survive the day in a daze than to try to subject herself to more than that. It seemed the only thing that helped her temporarily get out of her funk were her art lessons with Sophia. That little girl was such a joy to be around... of course it tended to be a bittersweet experience for Anna because she usually ended up thinking of Ezra afterwards, but she decided to take the bad with the good and reminded herself that she would likely be grieving for her son for the rest of her life. That didn't mean she couldn't enjoy her time with Sophia, though.

As she thought about that, the doorbell rang. She pulled her robe closed around herself and opened the front door.

"Are you Anna Reynolds?" a man in a suit asked her as she stood in the doorway with coffee in hand and an epic mess of brown hair crowning her half-awake face.

"Unfortunately," she replied. "What can I do for you?"

"I'm Special Agent Lowell," the man in front of her said. He motioned to his right. "This is my partner, Agent Jones. May we come in?"

Anna's skeptical expression and lack of response prompted a flash of FBI badges. Once she inspected them, she stepped aside with a confused look on her face.

"What can I do for you?" she asked. "Did something happen?"

"As a matter of fact—" Agent Jones began. Lowell cut him off.

"We're here to ask you some questions about Dr. Andrew Peterson."

"What about him?" she asked, a puzzled look crossing her face. "Is he okay?"

The agents exchanged a significant glance before Lowell began speaking again.

"Dr. Peterson's body was found—"

"What?!" Anna cut him off. "That's impossible! I just saw him yesterday!" she exclaimed. *This is way too much to handle at 9:00 AM,* she thought. *They have to be wrong!*

"We know," Lowell said.

"That's why we're here," Jones added.

Anna raked her free hand through her messy hair, shocked and with tears already welling up in her eyes. "How do you know that? And what happened?" she asked, not looking at the agents as she tried to wrap her head around what they were saying. "This cannot be happening," she muttered aloud. Anna wasn't ready to lose yet another person in her life.

The two men glanced at each other before looking at Anna, who had started pacing up and down the hallway, wandering almost to the kitchen and then back to where the agents stood in the entry.

"Well," Jones began.

"He was found in his home a couple of hours ago," Lowell continued. "We've opened an investigation due to his status and we believe there might be foul play involved. I don't think we should go into more detail than that, but we do need to ask you a few questions, if you don't mind," Lowell added.

Anna just nodded and wandered into the kitchen numbly, motioning for them to follow her. *There's no way he can really be dead. What the fuck?* she thought. Whether she wanted to admit it or not, she was disappointed at never getting to find out about her disease, but also about the relationship that had so much potential for her. This pain was different from the pain she'd felt when her little Ezra died....

"You have Morgellons," Jones stated hesitantly after she sat down. "Is that correct?"

Anna nodded. "So?"

"There have been some strange things happening around people with Morgellons in recent years. We're not completely sure if it's a coincidence or not, but we need to do our due diligence and find out as much as we can about those involved, directly as well as indirectly.

"Did Dr. Peterson say anything out of the ordinary to you before you parted ways yesterday?"

Anna reflected for a moment. The only thing they'd spoken about was her treatment and her physical. "Nothing of note," she replied. "I had a physical and he suggested a topical treatment."

"No strange statements or code?"

Anna snorted. "Code?" she asked.

"Alright. Well, has anything strange been happening to you?"

Anna paused. "No... I've been a little stressed and this isn't going to help that at all, but that's about all."

The agents exchanged a significant look.

"Thank you, Ms. Reynolds," Jones said. They began making their way back to the door, leaving Anna baffled, shocked, and ready to throw her half-empty coffee mug at one of their heads.

"Just a goddamn minute now," she said, anger quickly bubbling up inside her almost uncontrollably. She clenched both hands around her coffee mug, trying not to lose it. "What kind of significance does that have? And what's been going on that's so strange about Morgellons? Are you not supposed to answer *any* of my questions?" Her voice rose as she finished the last question.

"I'm sorry, Ms. Reynolds," Lowell said, a look of sympathy in his eyes. "We cannot discuss this any further. It's classified. But we'll be in touch if we need anything." He handed her a business card. "Please... if you remember anything out of the ordinary, give us a call."

They left as abruptly as they'd shown up, and Anna went back into the kitchen listlessly. Her anger had subsided, but she couldn't believe what she'd heard.

"Can he really be... *gone?*" she mumbled to herself, sadness hitting her and creating a strange heaviness in the pit of her stomach. Andrew had been her only friend in dealing with this disease. He had grown to mean a lot to her, and now he was just... gone. Her heart hurt and her thoughts alternated between disbelief and disappointment, mingling with flashbacks of the sheer agony she had experienced when Ezra died.

Past and present emotions intertwined in her heart and the pit of her stomach. She had tried for years not to think about her son's death too much, especially since it had led to Nolan leaving her, too. The two of them had extremely different grieving processes, which made the entire situation more complicated up until her ex-husband finally couldn't take it anymore and left her. Not that she could blame him....

And now she had to go through this whole shitty process again.

∞

Anna's sores weren't going away with the treatment Andrew had suggested. They would begin to heal and then open up again after more fibers appeared, rendering the process redundant. She figured it would be better to be repetitive than miserable and hopeless, though, so she continued the treatment while also doing more research on some things that might work and wouldn't require a doctor.

She essentially shut down for most of her days over the next several weeks, save for a few days a week when she would do some graphic design for clients to keep her finances in check. She was miserable and in mourning for a friendship, but also for a love that never had the chance to be. She felt uninspired and listless most of the time. At several points, she even prayed... something she hadn't done in years. She was angry that God kept taking people she cared about from her and even wondered if she could get Andrew back somehow, which of course was impossible.

Then, after several weeks of treating her wounds twice a day despite her varying cycles of depression and anger, they faded enough to be missed at a glance even though fibers were still being excreted. Anna wanted to do something special to celebrate her small victory and wished that Andrew was around to celebrate with her. However, she had allowed herself some time to not function, had been drinking way too much wine and sleeping entirely too much, and she knew that she had to get back to some semblance of a normal life soon. She decided to go out for a cup of coffee and sit with a book to read, something she hadn't done in a long time. Maybe she could pull herself out of the darkness and get back to living.

Anna considered calling Casey. Andrew's mysterious death was exactly the kind of thing she would love... or use as story fodder for a novel, especially since the FBI came to Anna's house. *I'd better not,* she thought. *It's been getting stranger and stranger, and I wouldn't want to put her in danger or worry her too much.*

Sighing as she plucked her keys out of a basket by the front door, she shook her head sadly and thought, *I hope you're there in spirit, Andrew. This might've been our first date in another life.*

For the most part, she tried to remember that he had been trying to help her with her health issues and that she would have to find another doctor who would be willing to do the same. The FBI showing up at her house was very strange, so she tried not to think too much about that, either, because conspiracy theories were a rabbit hole she didn't want to explore without more evidence first.

Anna arrived at the cafe and immediately felt her mood lifting. Before her illness became too obvious to hide, she would stop by this cafe whenever she could to sit and read for an hour or two, relaxing and enjoying a cup of coffee or tea. There was a small movie theater next door, so she was able to people-watch if she chose to.

Book in hand, Anna got out of her car and walked into the cafe, the smells of coffee beans and steamed milk making their way into her nostrils like one of those hand-shaped steam tendrils in cartoons. She only wished she could float to the counter, guided by that invisible hand made of delightful aromas.

After pausing to take in the pleasant smells, she walked over to order her favorite drink: a white chocolate mocha, no whip, with an extra shot at 130 degrees. She chose a seat toward the back of the cafe, in a corner so she could see what was happening around her and near a window so she could watch the moviegoers as they entered and exited the theater.

One of the things that she loved the most about this particular cafe was that it was furnished with mismatched couches and other furniture that looked restored, like it all had history and stories to tell if it could communicate. Grateful for a large padded chair, she curled herself up into it as if she lived there and prepared to get lost in her book.

After a few pages, she paused and took a few sips of her coffee. Though the whole idea of getting out had been to keep her mind off of her actual life and offer a brief distraction, she found herself lost in thought about Morgellons, Andrew's murder, and why in the world the FBI was interested in both.

How did he even die? They never bothered to tell me any details. And why would someone murder *Andrew?*

"Is this seat taken, miss?" a young man asked, gesturing to the large chair across from her. She smiled and nodded automatically, not really paying attention.

"Go ahead, no one's sitting there."

"Thanks," he said, sitting down. He held a large cup of coffee in his left hand and a book in his right. After sitting down, he opened his book to the last third, where he unfolded a dog-eared corner and read.

Anna watched him as she pretended to continue reading her own book. He was younger than she was, but well-dressed and handsome with dark hair and amber eyes. She always dog-eared the corners of her books, too, which was the first thing she noticed about him, save for his saying *miss* instead of *ma'am*.

He looked up at her face from his book and she quickly looked down at hers, hoping he wouldn't think she was weird.

"My name's James," he said after they'd continued their little eyeball game for a while. He smiled, held his hand out to her, and she shook it, smiling politely.

"Anna," she replied. "Nice to meet you."

"You, too," he said with a beaming smile. "You know, we're technically having coffee together, so we may as well have a little conversation to go along with it."

She smiled. "Okay, I'll bite... Why this cafe?"

"I like it... It's my favorite place to relax outside of my house. What about you?"

"Same... And I haven't been here in a long time."

"Can I ask why?"

Anna furrowed her brows. "Personal reasons," she stated.

"That's okay... I don't like to pry, anyway."

There was a pause.

"Do you want to go see a movie?" James asked suddenly. "The theater is right next door...."

Anna was surprised, but after a moment's consideration, she agreed, thinking, *why not?* She felt like it was time to shake things up a bit and encourage her emotions to go back toward the positive rather than wallowing all the time. She knew that she would have good days and bad days, but she wanted to make sure that her good days outweighed the bad, not vice versa. To do this, she knew she would have to take control of her emotions again. They both finished their coffee and walked out of the cafe's glass doors toward the movie theater.

The two of them enjoyed their time together, making jokes and talking a little throughout the movie. After it was done, they went outside and sat on the sidewalk against the wall of the theater.

"So, James," Anna began. "What do you do for a living?"

"I'm an intern at the hospital right now, trying to figure out what my specialty will be," he said with a smile.

Anna's eyes sparkled a little as she realized James was working at the hospital and around a number of doctors.

"Do you know Dr. Mitchell?" she asked, remembering her time at the hospital a few months earlier.

"I do, actually, just not well," James replied, then narrowed his eyes a little. "Doesn't he work in the psych ward?" Anna had not considered the implications of what she was asking before the words tumbled out of her mouth. She sighed, kicking herself for even bringing it up.

"He does," she replied simply.

"How do you know him?" James asked, intrigued.

"It's a really long story," she said sheepishly, not wanting to go into detail. Looking down, she picked at a hangnail and waited for James to change the subject, but he was interested now.

"I don't have to be anywhere," he said as he reached out and took her hand. "No judgment, okay? I'm just curious," he added. "Besides... I can always just ask Dr. Mitchell about you tomorrow," he said, half-joking. Anna rolled her eyes. She liked James, and she needed access to another doctor who would help her. Dr. Mitchell had been open to hearing about her condition and was the first person to not think she had some kind of delusion. He had been the one to help her connect with Andrew. If there was anyone who could find another doctor to work with her, it was Dr. Mitchell... through James.

Feeling more comfortable, Anna decided to open up about her affliction.

"You know how you asked me why I hadn't been here in so long?" she began. He nodded. "Well, it's because I have a rare condition that makes my skin do some pretty crazy things and I don't like being in public when that happens. It's not contagious," she added, knowing that some people could be extremely germ phobic. To her relief and slight surprise, he smiled.

"Well, that's that, then, isn't it?" he said. "Are you in treatment?" he asked with a genuine interest.

"I was... It was unofficial... but my doctor is no longer with us. But Dr. Mitchell was the one who informed my old doctor about me, which got the ball rolling in the first place. Before then it was all just guesswork and seeing what I could learn online."

James shot Anna a significant look and she nodded at him to confirm that the doctor being gone was taken as it had been meant.

"Well, that's not good," James said. "Are you going to a new doctor?" Anna simply shook her head. "I have a few connections at the hospital," James stated, looking sincerely concerned for her. "I can always talk to Dr. Mitchell on your behalf, see if he has any ideas for you. I'm sure he'll remember you if your condition is rare. What is it?"

Anna smiled at his gesture. "Thanks, James... but this is really not your problem, and most doctors scoff at this illness and claim that it's psychosomatic. I couldn't—"

"Don't worry," James cut her off. "I understand... but if Dr. Mitchell helped you before, considering the circumstances, I bet he would help you again."

Anna smiled. "Maybe," she said, wondering if there was still hope for her after all.

∞

Despite Anna's struggle to deal with everything, she knew she still had to give Sophia her art lessons. On one hand, she didn't want to see *anyone*, not even a child who made her smile more often than not. On the other, she welcomed the distraction. She knew her time with Sophia would make her feel better no matter what happened, so she resisted her grief-induced urge to cancel.

Before long, there was a knock at the door and Sophia greeted Anna with a glowing smile and a strange glimmer in her blue eyes. Anna sensed something darker than excitement, however.

"Hi, Sophia!" she greeted warmly and gave her little art prodigy a hug.

"Anna!" Sophia said animatedly. "I think I figured out what I remember that was making me feel so bad," she whispered with harsh excitement. Anna was taken aback slightly, but maintained her smile.

"Oh?" she asked. "What do you think it is?" she asked.

"I just found out that my dad works on people's insides," Sophia said, her dark excitement quickly replaced by a severe look of resentment and confusion. Anna furrowed her eyebrows.

"What do you mean, like surgery?" Anna asked with growing curiosity.

"He does things to people's code," Sophia said. Anna realized immediately what Sophia was talking about.

"Their code?" she asked. "Do you mean people's DNA?" Anna asked, trying to maintain an innocent approach. Sophia nodded urgently.

"I heard something in Dad's study last night and went to go look. I saw him watching me on the TV when I was really little and I looked like I was really sick and hurting. But it was all quiet and in black and white. While he was playing that, he was on the phone with someone talking about genetic... something, and that he hid something inside my code!" Sophia paused, her emotions catching up with her. "Does that mean my own dad was using me as a test person? Doing *experiments* on me?!" She let out a sob as Anna pulled her into an embrace, cradling her head in her arms against her stomach.

"*Shh*," Anna said softly, kissing Sophia on her head. "It's okay now, sweetheart," she said softly, her mind racing with alarming and disturbing questions about Dr. Schwartz... and what in the world he might be up to.

∞

Anna glanced at her alarm clock. 2:50 AM. She couldn't believe she was awake at this time of night. Rolling over and kicking her comforter to cover her legs, she closed her eyes and tried to let sleep take her again.

She was just getting to the point where sounds became distant and her body began sinking into the mattress when her eyes snapped open again. She felt someone in her room. Trying to stay still, she opened her eyes and peeked out at her bedroom.

There was no light, but she could still see some shadows in her room. It was at the back of the house, so she knew no vehicles could shine light into her room and play tricks on her vision.

As she watched intently, there was slow movement along the far wall. It moved beyond her vision as if it knew she wasn't sleeping. Anna had a decision to make.

Throwing her covers off, she jumped up into a kneeling position on her bed, turned her lamp on, and looked around the room shakily.

Nothing.

∞

The twinkling sound of the wind chimes gave an eerie undertone to the night, the wind blowing through the trees and the darkness seeming more intense than usual. Anna wrapped her coat tightly around herself, walking briskly back toward home. She usually didn't walk anywhere, especially at night, but she'd decided to get some fresh air and needed time to think. Walking was always good for that, even if it was a little cold and got dark somewhat early.

Reaching into her pocket for her keys, she approached the front door. The porch light was out – she must've forgotten to turn it on before she left. Trying to work through feeling alone and fending off paranoia in the overwhelming darkness, she rummaged in her purse for her keys and retrieved them just as her foot hit something on her front porch. Of course she couldn't see, but it sounded and felt like a box. *A package? I don't remember ordering anything....*

She pulled her cell phone out of her purse and turned on the flashlight app to see what was happening. Shining the light on her porch, she saw that it was, indeed, a box. *A mystery box,* she thought. *As if my life couldn't get any stranger.*

She unlocked the front door and flipped the light switch, but nothing happened. Trying to juggle her phone and the box at the same time, she walked into the house, set the box down, and went into the living room to try the light there. Also nothing. Shaking her head and doing her best to quiet her thoughts, she made her way into the garage with her phone and found the breaker box. She flipped the switch and the lights came on without a problem.

Things are getting entirely too weird around here, she thought, cautiously making her way back to her entry where the box sat. She switched off her flashlight app and stood still for a few moments, listening to see if she could hear anything to indicate that someone was in the house. She didn't think so because her door had been locked, but she was so scared she could hear her heartbeat pounding in her ears. Everything else was silent; she couldn't be completely sure, though, because her heart racing sounded so loud.

She made her way into the kitchen for a knife and then quietly snuck through her house to each room, checking for intruders. She had to be sure. If what the FBI guys had told her was true, Andrew was murdered in his own home, so there was no way she could ignore the possibility that someone might be after her, too. As she checked the last room and found no one, she let out a huge sigh of relief and took a few calming breaths to steady her heartbeat.

Satisfied that no one was in her house, she picked up the box and took it into her kitchen. She set it on the counter and inspected it. There was a note taped to the top. She unfolded it and read aloud, "Trust no one."

Trust no one? What is this?

Unsure of whether she should be expecting a severed head or a bomb, she opened the box carefully and looked inside.

Chapter Six

Files, journals, DVD+Rs, and what looked like a random note were what she found in the box. She recognized the two files as those that she'd seen in Andrew's desk filing drawer. *Jody and Anna,* she thought, opening her own file first. Just as she did, the phone rang.

"How have you been the past few days?" James' voice traveled through the phone to Anna's left ear. It had been several weeks since their first meeting and they had bumped into each other twice at the cafe. After they did, they exchanged numbers and he called to see how she was doing once every week or two.

"Okay, I guess... I've been waking up in the middle of the night... or at least I feel like I wake up... And just feeling totally groggy and weird, like I was drugged or something," she told him. As soon as she spoke the words she realized how crazy she sounded... again.

"That can't be good... have you thought about taking something to help you sleep?" he asked.

"Honestly?" Anna paused. "I've thought about it many times... But I'm a little afraid of sleeping pills. The thought of taking them makes me nervous."

"Understandable. What about a more natural approach? Like warm milk with honey or Valerian root? Even drinking some chamomile might help...."

"I drink chamomile all the time, but I'll try some of the others... I'd rather not take any pills, though."

"So what are you doing tomorrow?" James asked.

"Not much... Probably just working. What's up?"

"Can I introduce you to someone?" James sounded hopeful.

"Sure, I guess... who is it?"

"A doctor friend of mine," James replied. "He has a vested interest in Morgellons. I'm not sure what the details are, but I guess someone in his family has it, too."

Anna considered it for a moment. "Sure. Where would you want to meet?"

"We can do the coffee shop, like always. I want you to be comfortable, though, so why don't you decide?"

"Well, I honestly don't want to leave the house. I wouldn't mind if you brought him here... I could make dinner." She smiled, wondering if things were finally going to get better again.

"Okay," he replied. "We can do that. What time do you want us to show up?"

Anna did some quick calculations in her head for food preparation time and replied, "Let's say at about six. That should give me enough time to make sure dinner is ready."

"Great! We'll see you at six tomorrow."

"Alright, see you then."

∞

The next day, Anna showered in the afternoon before she made dinner. Her mood was lifted, as meeting a new doctor would surely yield some kind of results. Andrew had gotten somewhere, though his efforts were short-lived. Anna frowned guiltily at her own thoughts. *I really miss him,* she thought, remembering how immediately he had been willing to be there for her, even if she did call him at four in the morning.

Once she freshened up, she went back downstairs to begin cooking. As she went through the motions of making dinner for more than one person, she found it to be therapeutic. She still didn't know what to make of Andrew's sudden death and the FBI stopping by. They hadn't shown up again, but even once seemed like a bad sign. Maybe there was something about Morgellons that she didn't know? Those agents had been pretty cryptic about the whole thing. And what about that box?

She mulled this over in her mind as she set the table and waited for the food to cook, stirring and seasoning as necessary. It was strange, the timing of everything. She didn't like that and paranoia began to settle in, so she tried to talk herself down. The thoughts were there, though, and she couldn't really stop those.

What if the government is secretly experimenting on people, giving them Morgellons for some kind of study or something? she wondered. *It's possible... what if they're trying to do experiments on people and the side-effect is Morgellons?* She stopped what she was doing. *What if they killed Andrew because he got too close to the truth?!*

Shaking her head as if to shake her thoughts loose, she finished setting the table and placed dinner in the center of the round tabletop. Because she still had a little bit of time, she decided to open the box again and rifle through it to see what she could find.

Carefully, she opened the flaps of the box. In the bottom, a worn piece of paper had a message scrawled on it, which Anna squinted at to make out what it said.

I can't take it anymore.
They have to find another subject.
The crawling is driving me mad!
Andrew... please forgive me.
Jody

"Who is Jody?" Anna muttered out loud as she opened an envelope with a stack of papers in it. She was surprised to see notes about Morgellons, information about herself, and treatment notes. There were some she didn't understand. It almost looked like someone had copied her medical file and delivered it to her.

One thing that caught her attention was a note scrawled in horrible handwriting about Anna's inability to sleep right. It seemed to be pointing out something about the fibers.

There was a loud knock at the door and Anna nearly jumped out of her skin. Scrambling to shove everything back into the box, she stuffed the whole thing into a lower cabinet in the kitchen, pulling plastic containers in front of it to conceal it as well as possible. The note from on top of the box was still out on the counter. Haphazardly folding it, she shoved it into her back pocket and rushed to the door, hoping the time it took her to answer didn't seem suspicious.

Smiling brightly, she opened the door to James and another man, both of them smiling as well.

"Hi, Anna," James said as she motioned for them to come in and held the door open.

"Hi, James," she said cheerfully, wondering if the note warning not to trust anyone meant him, too. Was she really all alone in this? Obviously she had *someone* wanting to help her, but who? And why all the mystery with the box and the note? The cryptic games and messages were just adding to her paranoia.

"This is my friend, Jonah," James said, gesturing toward the older gentleman next to him. Anna shook his hand confidently and smiled, hoping that James wouldn't notice her nervousness.

"Hi, Anna," Jonah said, returning the handshake and smiling.

"It's nice to meet you. James has told me about your condition. I look forward to being able to help you, or at least give you hope regarding treatment." He paused. "Let's see if we can make some progress."

Anna smiled again, nodding her thanks. "I hope so, too," she said. "But for now, let's eat." Leading the way, she walked to the kitchen and motioned for each of them to take their seats. Once they did, she walked back to get a bottle of wine and three glasses. When she returned to the dining room, the two were whispering about something but stopped abruptly when she entered. *Trust no one*, a little voice in the back of her mind said. She tried to ignore it. Smiling, they graciously accepted their glasses and Jonah opened the bottle.

Anna took her seat and uncovered mashed potatoes, gravy, and some chicken vegetable stir-fry she'd whipped up. After dishing up and taking several bites, the three of them began talking.

"So, Anna," Jonah began, "can you tell me how long you've suffered from Morgellons?" He paused and added, "This is terrific, by the way. My compliments to the chef." He smiled and took another bite.

"Thank you," Anna replied, returning the smile. "As far as the Morgellons, I first started noticing it several months ago. I thought it was an allergic reaction to my detergent or something."

"And would you say it's gotten progressively worse?" he asked. James listened and ate quietly.

Anna paused, contemplating the question's relevance. "Well, yes... I guess you could say it has. Or I'm just noticing it more, I don't know. The loss of sleep is what's really bothering me because I feel groggy a lot."

"Alright." Jonah paused to take another bite. "I have a couple of ideas that might help. I don't know how well any of them will work, but they're worth a try."

"Agreed," Anna replied with a smile.

They ate in silence for several moments. She noted that Jonah seemed to be a bit older than she and James were, with graying hair and blue eyes. She guessed that he was in his mid-fifties.

"So, James," Anna began, breaking the silence. "How do you know Jonah?"

Jonah gave James a strange look Anna wasn't sure what to make of.

"Well," James began, then took a sip of his wine. "We work

together at the hospital," he stated.

"Right," Anna nodded. "I should have gathered that," she added.

"Oh, no worries. You're a wonderful cook, Anna," James said.

"Thanks," she replied. She was sensing some awkwardness, like maybe they didn't know each other as well as they were trying to have her believe.

They continued their meal without speaking. Jonah sipped his wine, having finished his dinner. James seemed lost in his own world. Anna refilled her wine and tried to ignore the suspicion and fog that was starting to take over her thoughts. Her vision blurred slightly and she blinked it away.

"Are you two okay?" she asked. They both turned their heads toward her and nodded.

"Fine," Jonah said.

"I'm great," James added.

"Are *you* okay?" James asked her, watching her intently.

"Yea," she replied. "I just feel very strange," she added. "Something's wrong...."

Anna felt groggy, like she usually did when she woke up in the middle of the night to the shadowy silhouettes surrounding her.

Jonah jumped up from his chair. "Anna?" he said loudly, alarmed. James continued to eat as if he hadn't noticed. Anna's eyes flickered, near blacking out. She tried to say something but her mouth wasn't working.

Suddenly she was falling. There was an arm behind her head and then nothing.

∞

"Make sure she's comfortable," James told Jonah authoritatively. "This should only take me a few minutes." Jonah nodded and left to find a pillow for the unconscious Anna as James took out a small zippered case from his inside coat pocket.

James pulled up both of her sleeves and inspected the sores on her arms, pleased to find that several new fibers had protruded and were ready to be collected. He took out some tweezers, his hands working quickly and precisely.

As he began pulling the fibers from her skin, Anna mumbled

incoherently.

"Don't worry, Anna," he told her in a soothing tone. "This won't take long and you're going to be just fine." He pulled gingerly on the fibers and gently exposed a small cluster of them, like fuzz on a coat. "You're serving the greater good right now," he mumbled as he worked on the next wound.

Jonah came back with a pillow and placed it under Anna's head gently.

"How long do you think she'll be out for?" Jonah asked James, who shrugged his shoulders.

"It could be seconds or minutes longer," he replied. He sighed and worked faster, gently putting all of the fibers into a small plastic zippered bag. He would have to put them into vials later.

"Okay," he said after another few moments. "I'm finished. Can you pull her sleeves back down?" Jonah nodded and did as he was asked while James zipped the bag and quickly placed it and the tweezers back in their case. As soon as the case was tucked neatly back in his coat pocket, Jonah began reviving Anna.

∞

"What's happening?" Anna heard herself say, sounding disconnected from her own body. She opened her eyes to try to get her bearings and her vision was blurred. Looking ahead, she realized there were shadowy silhouettes around her. She counted four, but she could've been hallucinating.

"Anna?" a voice said through the fog. "Anna? It's Jonah. Are you okay?" He sounded distant and muffled.

"What happened?" She heard herself more clearly now and her vision started to return to normal.

"You fainted," James replied. Both men had moved from their chairs to either side of her, the doctor checking her pulse and touching her forehead. She felt a pillow under her head, but the floor under the rest of her body was hard and cold. She shivered.

"How do you feel?" Jonah asked with concern in his eyes.

"I'm f-freezing," she replied, attempting to sit up so she could get off of the kitchen floor. Jonah blocked her gently with his arm.

"I wouldn't try to get up so fast if I were you," he said. He reached into his pocket and pulled out a small flashlight. He nodded at

James and the men helped her sit up against the base of the kitchen island.

Anna squeezed her eyes shut as Jonah shone the light into them.

"You're gonna have to let me check your pupils," he said, failing to stifle a bemused smile. "You are a stubborn woman, you know that?" Anna raised an eyebrow and opened one eye reluctantly to look at him.

"What's that supposed to mean?"

"When you fainted I barely caught you in time.... You've been muttering nonsense and trying to push us away from you the whole time we've been trying to help you," he added.

"Yea, I guess that sounds like me," she replied, smiling back and opening both eyes. Though the light was uncomfortable at first, she let the doctor check her and tried to relax. James handed her a glass of water.

"Well, it doesn't look like you did any damage," Jonah said as he clicked off the flashlight and shoved it back into his pocket. "Does this happen often?" he asked, almost as an afterthought. Anna noticed, but didn't know what to make of that in her still-groggy brain.

"Not like that," Anna replied, furrowing her brows as she sucked down the glass of cool water. "Thank you," she told James as he set the empty glass on the table.

"Well, if not like that then how?" Jonah asked, giving her another look of concern.

"Usually I'm already sleeping and I just wake up feeling groggy like I just did.... It's just not normal."

"No kidding it's not normal," Jonah said. "But I need to know more about how this has been happening so maybe I can help you to stop it from happening again. Especially if it's happening during your waking hours. I mean… it would be a disaster if you were to try to drive anywhere and suddenly fainted at the wheel."

Anna nodded solemnly. "So... what should we do?" she asked the doctor.

"We'll have to run some tests and I'll need to figure out why you're having such odd symptoms. I've never seen a Morgellons sufferer randomly passing out before, so I'd like to see if you have any other underlying conditions. How do you feel about that?"

"That's fine with me," she said, and the two men helped her to her feet. "I just want it to stop," she added.

"Do you want help to your bed or the couch?" James asked, still holding on to her arm. She nodded.

"Let me just stay on the couch tonight," she said. "It's closer to everything," she added with a smile.

James and Jonah led her to the oversized couch in the living room and handed her the remote from on top of the entertainment shelf.

"On that note," James said, jumping to his feet, "I think it's time for us to get out of here, don't you?"

Jonah nodded. As he stood, he handed her a business card.

"Give me a call to set up a proper appointment. I can come here if you'd like. We'll discuss the particulars later."

"Do you need anything else, Anna?" James asked. She smiled from the couch and shook her head.

"I'm just going to rest here for a while and then head up to bed." She pulled the blanket – a permanent fixture on the couch – over herself and snuggled into the soft cushions.

"Stay there for at least an hour," Jonah said, pausing in the doorway to look back at her. "I don't want you to hurt yourself."

"Will do," she said. "Sorry about that... I hope you have a good night! Thanks for coming to dinner." Jonah nodded again and disappeared to the entryway. Anna heard the door shut and fell asleep, unsure of what to make of her sudden narcolepsy... or their sudden departure.

∞

The next day, Anna felt a little stiff from sleeping on the couch but decided to get the ball rolling. She found the business card Jonah had given her and saw that his cell phone number was scrawled on the back.

"Jonah Miller," she mumbled as she dialed his office number as listed on the business card. After two rings, a woman with a pleasant voice answered the phone.

"Doctor Miller's office, this is Sally. How can I help you?"

"Hi," Anna began with a slight smile. "I'm calling for Doctor Miller. Is he available? This is Anna Reynolds." She fiddled with the business card as she spoke.

"I'm sorry, he's with a patient at the moment. Can I take down your number and have him call you back?" Sally asked. Anna could hear the smile in the receptionist's voice. This was something she'd begun noticing after a brief stint of working in a call center.

"Sure, that works." She gave the woman her phone number and hung up, slipping back into feeling stuck.

Anna wasn't sure what to do with herself. It wasn't that she was depressed or anything... not today. She just felt blah... unmotivated. She paced around the living room for a while, sat on the couch, got back up, paced some more, and finally laid back down and turned on the TV. Maybe some shows about fictional problems would distract her from her own.

After several TV shows and several more cups of coffee, the phone rang. She picked it up immediately.

"Hello?"

"Anna?"

"Yes?"

"This is Jonah. How are you feeling today?" Anna smiled.

"I'm fine... a little restless, but fine. How are you?"

"I'm doing well. What can I help you with? You called earlier," he said.

"Well, I was wondering if you would be able to schedule an appointment with me at my house," she said. Jonah chuckled.

"Of course. I think I'm free on Wednesday at about two in the afternoon. Does that work for you?"

Anna smiled. "Yes it does," she replied.

"Great. I'll see you then, okay?" Anna agreed and they hung up.

Feeling a million times better about her day, Anna decided it was time to get some client work done and do some cleaning. The dinner mess from the night before wouldn't scrub itself, unfortunately.

As she began to gather dishes and pile them into the dishwasher, her thoughts wandered back to the mystery box that had appeared on her doorstep. She knew she had to get some things done before she could allow herself to sit down and study the contents, so she finished loading the dishwasher and ran it, quietly appreciating the hum of the appliance at work.

She checked her email to see if there were any urgent messages from her clients so she could properly prioritize her day. But that stupid box kept tugging at her brain, begging her to open it up and take a thorough look at what was inside. Unable to concentrate, she gave in to her mind's incessant nagging.

She took the box out from behind the plastic containers in the cabinet and pulled out a manila folder with a file in it that looked like someone's medical record. It looked very similar to the other file in the box with Anna's name on it. This one, though, didn't belong to her. It belonged to Jody Smith.

Anna paused and furrowed her brow. She began flipping through the various papers in the file. Morgellons was there toward the end of it, along with severe anxiety and depression. That was when Anna remembered the note she had haphazardly stuffed in her pants pocket the night before. She jumped up and ran upstairs to pull those jeans out of her hamper and retrieve the note.

It was crumpled, but still legible.

I can't take it anymore.
They have to find another subject.
The crawling is driving me mad!
Andrew... please forgive me.
—Jody

Who is Jody? Anna wondered again. The note sounded pretty cryptic. *Who are 'they?' And what was her relationship with Andrew?* Anna knew there were connections that she wasn't making, but what could she do other than read, research, and keep trying to treat her mysterious disease? Anna had no idea why this box was dropped on her doorstep or by whom.

Nevertheless, she kept digging through it.

Among the contents were several samples of Morgellons fibers with labels on them. Some of them said Jody Smith while others were labeled Anna Reynolds. Both also had some kind of handwritten reference number on them, which Anna had no idea what to make of.

In the very bottom of the box was an old black and white composition notebook that was tattered and worn off around the edges. The front cover was simply labeled, 'Research.'

Pulling the notebook from the box, Anna could tell it had been used, abused, and studied at great length. She gingerly opened the front cover and slowly scanned through the first several pages of scrawled handwriting, which she could barely read.

She got about a third of the way into the notebook when the

writing became much more legible. It was as if something drastic had happened and the writing went from a stressed out scrawl to a calm and more deliberate hand.

> *Jody killed herself yesterday. I'm not sure why I'm writing this in my research notebook, but I suppose it's because this might be part of the research. I don't know what it means, and I know I'm still in shock and haven't processed the loss yet. Her note was so cryptic and doesn't make any sense. It was written specifically to me, but whose subject was she if she wasn't mine? Was someone experimenting on her?*

Anna's hand covered her mouth as she realized that this was Andrew's notebook. She wasn't sure what to make of this new information, either, but her heart went out to the Andrew who had written this in his grief and still remained focused on finding out what Morgellons was and developing a cure.

> *My findings have mostly led nowhere. All I know is that this disease, Morgellons, has massive negative effects on its sufferers and isn't easy to control or cure. It seems like Jody just started losing her mind, but I knew her – she wasn't crazy. I think there was more going on than initially meets the eye.*
>
> *The only problem is that if I tell anyone about this, I might wind up in a mental institution and lose my job. So I guess I'll just have to write it all down.*

Anna continued to flip through the notebook, hoping to learn more. At the halfway point, the writing became more frantic again, but she could still read it. To her surprise, it was about her.

> *I've found a new patient with Morgellons. I know it's a little odd for me to seek out people with this disease, but hopefully she doesn't see it that way. Her name is Anna Reynolds and her story is pretty interesting so far.*
>
> *As I suspected before, I would probably be institutionalized if I came forward to anyone with this. Anna actually was institutionalized in the hospital. They can keep her for 72 hours if they feel she is a danger to herself or others, but that rule is abused constantly.*
>
> *I heard about her from a colleague in the psych ward who also*

informed me about a specimen she'd brought in that she supposedly pulled out of her tear duct. That in and of itself is an interesting aspect to her story. I've never seen or heard of anyone pulling a fiber clump out of their eye, and it intrigued me, too, because it must have been painful. As I suspected, she seems to be a mentally and emotionally tough woman.

I retrieved the clump of fibers from the lab almost immediately and was in pain just imagining pulling something that size out of my tear duct. What really surprised me is that she didn't have a sore in her eye before the fibers appeared. They just simply came out of her tear duct.

Upon speaking to her about it, I found out she pulled it out herself in her bathroom at home. I did notice that her eyes were rimmed with what looked like slight bruising when I met her, so that confirms that she was determined to get whatever foreign item this was out of herself no matter how painful it might be.

I sincerely hope that I can help this woman and that she doesn't go crazy like Jody did, although I am still in doubt that this was what happened.

The important part is that I now have another patient to study and will hopefully be able to find a cure. I'm working with a couple of other people on this, but they don't seem to be as interested in finding a cure as I am. But I hope, with the specimens I'm able to get from Anna, that either they or I will be able to find some kind of cure for this strange disease.

Working with other people? Anna thought, furrowing her brows. *How come he never mentioned that to me? I thought it was just him.* Anna sighed and closed the notebook, placing it back in the box. She had plenty of time to read through the rest of it later, although she didn't know if she would like what she found.

∞

Anna restlessly tidied up as she waited for Dr. Miller to get to her house for her appointment. She wasn't sure what to expect this time since he was a different doctor and she didn't know if he would share Andrew's passion for trying to find a cure, but she had to give it a shot. At least he had listened to her and *not* thrown her back into the psych ward.

Over the course of several days, she'd been able to go through most of the items in the box, completely neglecting her client work and becoming obsessed with what it all might mean and why there were so many strange aspects to Morgellons. She still couldn't explain that part and it started messing with her.

She promised herself she wouldn't go crazy for real, but with all the mystery surrounding this disease, she couldn't help but entertain the idea that there may, in fact, be something more going on beneath the surface of what was readily available to learn about the condition.

The phone rang at 1:59 PM and Anna answered it, wondering who it might be.

"Anna? It's Casey," her best friend's voice said on the other end. Anna smiled.

"Hey! How are you? I feel like we haven't talked in ages," she said, partially excited and partially jittery.

"Oh, I'm good… busy, as usual, but I have a spare minute so I wanted to call and ask if you want to come over and have dinner next weekend? Nothing fancy, just me, you, and the kids. And possibly a date," she added coyly.

"A date?" Anna asked with a grin. "Who might the lucky guy be?"

As Casey began to answer, Anna's doorbell rang. *Of course*, she thought. *Why, life? Why do you do these things?* Anna missed talking to her friend.

"I'm so sorry, Casey," Anna said into the receiver as she opened her front door.

"What's going on?" Casey asked, unoffended by the interruption. She had three kids, so she was accustomed to interruptions.

"I actually have a doctor's appointment right now and he just got here," Anna said haphazardly, motioning for Jonah to come in. He took his coat off and smiled at her as she finished her conversation.

"Oh, really?" Casey said, her voice mischievous. "You should bring him to dinner next Sunday, then," she said quickly and hung up. Anna burst out laughing, adoring her friend's style. Shaking her head, she hung up her phone and ushered Jonah into the dining room.

"What's so funny?" he asked her, genuinely curious. She chuckled again and shook her head.

"My friend, Casey…. She's just a goofball, that's all," she said. "Are we ready to get started?"

"Of course," Jonah replied, sitting down at the table with his bag. "I'd like to do a series of tests once I check your vitals. Some of these are blood tests. Are you squeamish about getting your blood drawn?"

"Not at all," Anna said, already rolling up her sleeve. She'd had quite a bit of coffee that morning and wondered if that was contributing to her nerves. Jonah chuckled as he watched her.

"There's no need to be nervous, you know," he told her reassuringly. "If you feel uncomfortable at any point, just let me know and we can come back to the process. Are you hydrated?"

"Sorry," Anna said a little sheepishly. "I think between the amount of coffee I had today and you being a new doctor, I'm feeling a little antsy. To answer your question, yes... I've had about four glasses of water since I stopped this morning's coffee madness," she said. He let out a small laugh.

"Sounds to me like your friend isn't the only goofball," he said, smiling. "Alright, first things first. I need to check your vitals, and then we can move on to collecting Morgellons samples and blood samples. Nothing invasive or too uncomfortable for the time being; I'd just like to take them back to the lab to see what I'm looking at and run a spectrum of tests."

"That sounds perfectly fine to me," she replied. Jonah got to work and they continued their polite small talk as he went about his task. Anna found herself missing Andrew as she watched Jonah work. Jonah was older and looked like he might retire at any time. Anna could tell that he was probably attractive once upon a time, but life had given him graying hair and lined his face quite a bit. His eyes were warm and friendly, but there was something there that she couldn't quite interpret.

Anna shrugged it off and let her mind wander back to Andrew. She had truly hoped that their bonding over Morgellons would lead to something more. *And it might have... if he were still alive,* she thought. She was disappointed and then felt guilty for only thinking of herself. Anna silently vowed to never hide her feelings toward anyone she felt a connection with again because it was better to get it out in the open and find out what might happen than to harbor those feelings and let them drive her crazy.

Andrew was dead. She felt like she hadn't even had time to mourn him because of all the craziness going on. Between the FBI showing up at her house, the box, and random fainting spells, she never had a chance to just sit down and cry, and even when she did have a moment, she pushed the sadness away, not allowing it to take over her thoughts.

"Are you okay, Anna?" Jonah asked with concern furrowing his brows. Anna snapped back to reality, shaking her head and sniffling as she realized that tears were falling from her eyes.

"Yea," she said as she wiped her tears away with her fingers. "I'm fine," she lied.

"Are you sure?" Jonah asked. "You don't seem fine. I didn't hurt you, did I?" Anna shook her head, no.

"No...." She hesitated. "I'm just... overwhelmed with everything going on," she said, remembering the note from on top of the mystery box. *Trust no one.*

"That's understandable," Jonah replied with a sympathetic look. "I'm all finished here... do you want to talk about it, or would you like me to leave?"

"I'm sure you have other patients to get to," she said with a watery smile. "I'll be fine," she added.

"Alright," Jonah said. He placed his hand over hers briefly and added, "Hang in there, kiddo."

"Thanks," she said with a chuckle.

As he left, Anna tried to hold it together as well as she could until she heard the front door close. She barely made it, her expression crumbling into silent sobs the second he was gone. Before long, she gasped for air, covering her face with her hands and letting it out.

She missed Andrew.

She didn't want to have to face this alone. She needed a chance to not have to be so strong all the fucking time. But then there was the note....

Trust no one.

Her strength was all she had.

∞

Anna's dreams were a muddled mess of spaceships, strange creatures, and the sensation of trying to find or retrieve something without any luck. But she'd followed all the clues....

She sat up in bed abruptly, catching eerie shadows moving along her walls before they vanished. The clock glowed 4:58 in bright red digital luminescence. As Anna blinked, she kept looking at the shadows on her walls. They seemed to be moving and she wasn't sure what they belonged to. It was creepy, but she dismissed it as paranoia at first... until the shadow she was looking at directly moved behind her dresser right before her eyes. Her heart rate quickened.

Anna slid out of bed quietly, wrapping her housecoat around herself. There was no source of immediate light from her window, only a slight crack of light from the hallway because her door was ajar. Her eyes hadn't needed to adjust to the dark; she had no trouble seeing. Had she imagined it?

As she softly made her way to the bedroom door, she felt the hair on the back of her neck and arms stand on end, like someone was watching her every move. Had someone broken into her house? Was that what woke her this early in the morning?

What did that shadow belong to?

She took a shaky breath, doing what she knew she had to despite her fear telling her to run from her bedroom as fast as she could and grab a knife from the kitchen.

She reached the bedroom door and flung it open, then turned on the light.

Nothing... as always.

Chapter Seven

Anna stared intently at the computer screen as she applied for several projects she could do to sustain her financial independence. With all the upheaval, she'd all but stopped working and it was beginning to show in her bank account. Today, she made up her mind to be more motivated and let her disease as well as losing Andrew bother her less. She figured she was seeing a doctor regularly and didn't have to worry so much about it. She'd let him do that for her.

Though the circumstances surrounding this disease were odd, Anna felt it was still her duty to herself to continue working and allot a certain amount of time every day to do research and pore over the contents of the box. She knew she couldn't survive without a paycheck and she also knew she would drive herself completely crazy if she continued to obsess over Morgellons and that box. It had to be more balanced so she wouldn't *actually* lose her mind.

It was the shadows that were really freaking her out, though. She didn't want to think about them.

Sighing, she took another sip of coffee and skimmed through the freelance site to find projects she wanted to work on. She'd been using the same sites to find work for years and there were usually some pretty good projects to apply for. She hadn't had any issues obtaining work there before, so it came as a bit of a surprise when all she found were projects that either paid too little for too much work or projects that didn't fit her skill set.

She closed her laptop after an hour of searching, deciding it would be better to try again the next day. Anna got up and wandered into the living room, plopping down on her huge, comfortable couch and turning on the TV. She had decided to stay away from the box of research for at least another hour, so she needed to do something to pass the time. Though she'd considered going upstairs to do some painting, she wasn't sure if she wanted to. She was feeling pretty bland and unmotivated.

Sighing again after channel surfing for a while, she turned the TV off and just sat there for a minute. Her mind wandered back to Andrew, as it did so often. Of course that made her think of the box and Andrew's notebook that was still hidden in a cabinet in the kitchen.

Letting out a little groan of frustration, she got up abruptly and stalked into the kitchen, opening the cabinet door and pulling out the box. She went immediately for the composition notebook and began reading it again to see if there was anything she was missing or hadn't gotten to yet.

It had been a while since the box appeared on her doorstep and she still didn't know how it got there in the first place. Turning a page in the notebook, she was surprised that there were several pages stuck together toward the back.

I never noticed that before, she thought as she tried to peel one of the pages apart from the rest. It looked like there were at least six or seven pages stuck together. As she peeled, the paper ripped and she stopped immediately. Ripped paper wouldn't do her any good if she wanted to find out what was written on it.

Taking the entire notebook with her, she prayed that the ink would stay put. It looked like the pages had been glued together on purpose in order to hide something; she could see where the glue had been applied. The writing looked like it was in regular ballpoint pen, so it wouldn't smear too much if she put the paper in warm water to soften the glue and get the pages to separate. She couldn't dry the pages properly if they were still in the notebook, so she grabbed a pair of scissors and cut out the pages as close to the book's seam as she could. The condition of the paper wouldn't make any difference; she just needed to see what had been written there.

Once she got the pages out of the book, she laid out a long sheet of wax paper to put the pages on as they dried. She filled the sink with warm water and began painstakingly soaking the bunch of pages in the sink, hoping they wouldn't get too damaged to read.

Gingerly, she pried each page apart from the stack and set the now-soaked paper one sheet at a time on the long sheet of wax paper. Her hope was that the wax paper would allow the other paper to dry without getting stuck.

Anna had been so engrossed in what she was doing that she nearly jumped out of her skin when her phone rang. Taking in a deep breath, she dried her hands and answered it.

"Hello?" Anna said.

There was static on the other end, making her nervous.

"Who is this?" she asked. "I can't hear you, so I'm hanging up. If it's important, please call back."

She hung up the phone only to have it ring again a moment

later. She checked the caller ID and it just said, 'unknown.'

"Hello?" she said again, this time unsure if she should be afraid or angry. It was static again, only this time she could make out the sound of someone breathing.

"If you have something to say to me, please say it," she said, keeping her tone even.

"Be careful," a male voice stated and hung up. Anna looked at her phone for a moment, not sure what to think. Was this person trying to harm her or help her? Or maybe just freak her out? If it was the latter, they succeeded incredibly well.

Anna shook her head, put the phone back on the counter, and continued to tend to her paper mess. By the time she finished, she had about ten pages laid out on wax paper, all drying.

What a pain, she thought with a slight smile, proud of her display of patience. Once she had set up a lamp, she began poring over the pages to see if anything was legible. She was dying to know what had been hidden there and wondered who had meant for her to find out.

The FBI approached me today to ask if I would participate in some kind of ongoing investigation into Morgellons. I initially said no, as I felt that it might be a breach between myself and my patient, but when they told me what they were doing I was intrigued and thought it might be helpful to get involved.

Apparently the FBI has a vested interest in the fibers and is searching for people to collect sample specimens for the purpose of study at a higher level. I can't be sure what the government's interest is in this disease, but I'm sure people like me could use the help in finding out what's causing it and hopefully coming up with a cure.

Of course the details of these studies are classified – go figure – but they did mention that they were studying the fibers in-depth and reaching out for more specimens for the time being, as well as basic overviews on how patients behave. Since Jody has Morgellons and would have a say in whether she wants her fibers used for research, I asked them if it would be okay to run this by her first.

That was when they informed me that each fiber specimen collected would be paid for. They must really be onto something in order to be willing to pay for their samples. The price range they gave me was $500 to $5,000 for each sample, depending on how many fibers were in a cluster *or if it was just a single strand. I find that offer to be extremely high, especially for something as expensive as research. That makes me wonder what else is going on that they can't tell me about.*

I ran it by Jody and she agreed to participate, if for no other reason than to have help with research and get some extra money. With her condition, she hasn't been able to return to work because people don't understand it. They think it's contagious and most people tend to completely avoid her. She just couldn't take that kind of treatment at work anymore, and who can blame her? Now all she has is me and those damned fibers. If we can make progress in our research and make some money at the same time, why not go for it?

Anna paused, her heart going out to this woman. She felt a pang in her chest when she remembered once again that both Jody and Andrew were dead.

We decided to go ahead and give them the first sample specimen of Jody's fibers today and were paid $3,000. Not a bad paycheck, all things considered. We worked pretty hard trying to remove this particular cluster from her skin without damaging anything, and it paid off well.

I'm really worried about her, though. I don't know how much more of this disease she can handle before she goes nuts. She's been having nightmares again and wakes up in a sweat, heart racing and her skin clammy. These dreams must be scaring the hell out of her, and there's nothing I can do about it. I feel so helpless.

On another note, I've been working on a combination of certain ingredients from nature that might help her skin heal. We've already tried several things, but this time I combined aloe gel with diatomaceous earth to see if it would make a difference. If this doesn't show any results, I'll try adding tea tree oil to it and see if it helps.

I don't want to use anything chemical on her skin as it's already irritated enough. I need to find more ingredients that are soothing, not harsh chemicals. I don't want to make it worse.

Anna moved on to another drying page on her kitchen counter. She wondered if anything had come of the samples they'd given to the FBI.

I spoke to the agent today to see where we stood and if they needed more samples yet. He said they always need more samples but hadn't found anything conclusive yet that would help them cure the disease. Something about his body language was off, though. I think there's a lot more going on here than we know.

Anna wondered about the FBI's involvement, too. Why would the government have such an interest in a disease that only affected 50,000 people? Granted the numbers may not have been accurate, but why would they show such a major interest in it? Especially if it essentially made the government and research facilities hemorrhage money the way it seemed like it was doing. Something just wasn't adding up.

I was recently made aware of a group called the Bureau of Quantum Sciences. Apparently this privately funded group is behind the government in their involvement with Morgellons and the unclear research they're conducting on these fibers.

I probably shouldn't be writing any of this down, but I feel that if I don't, the information may not be safe in my head. Aside from that, if something happens to me, then I can easily give this knowledge to someone else who can make use of it. That's my hope, anyway.

There have been agents outside our home for several days now, just watching. I honestly have no idea what to make of that, but I do know that it's making Jody and me... uncomfortable, to say the least. I wonder now if we shouldn't have agreed to participate in this so-called research after all. But I guess what's done is done and we'll just have to keep moving forward. The money is a nice bonus and we've been able to build a little cushion in our savings account, so hopefully they'll decide that we've given them enough and leave us alone. Maybe I'll just ask them to go away, that we're not interested anymore.

It just all seems so surreal.

Anna stopped reading there. "Bureau of Quantum Sciences?" she mumbled aloud. "What the fuck is *that?*"

Making her way back to the other side of the kitchen island, she started digging through the box again in hopes that she would find something useful. She went back into her medical records and laid them out beside Jody's. Anna was fairly certain that if she got caught with these she would be arrested, but she had to keep digging.

Searching online would be too risky since everything can be monitored, so she knew she would have to learn more from the materials at hand.

As she looked through the medical records to compare, she found certain forms intermittently that were almost exactly the same in both records. Going to the first instance of each form in the folders, Anna read them and found that they were essentially to document Morgellons, although they each followed another similar document stating that the ailment was delusional parasitosis.

That must be about the time Andrew came into the picture, Anna thought. She continued looking through the paperwork, arriving at the second instance of the same form in both records.

At the bottom of each of these forms, there was a little note that said, "Harvested specimen donated for research." Anna was baffled, especially by that same statement being on the form stating the disease was psychological. If it was psychological, why would they donate anything to research? Why would they even humor the potential existence of any physical manifestations of this disease if they were claiming it was a delusion? And then another question... why did it say the specimens were donated when they were essentially sold for profit?

Anna let out a huge sigh, frustrated and her head pounding with unanswered questions. She decided it was time to put all of this away and wind down.

∞

When Anna heard a knock on her door the next afternoon, she was in the middle of a project and covered in various shades of acrylic paint. Trying to wipe her hands on her apron, she made her way to the front door only to be surprised by James and Jonah's smiling faces.

"Well, hello," she said, wondering what they were doing at her house unannounced.

"Hello, Anna," Jonah said, reaching out to shake her hand in greeting and chuckling at the paint on hers. "How have you been feeling?" he asked.

"Not too bad today, actually," she replied. "I've been kind of pouring myself into various projects to stay busy and distracted," she added. "Would you like to come in?" She gestured for them to enter the house.

"So, what brings you by today?" she asked. "I thought you forgot about me," she added jokingly to James, who hadn't been calling her like he used to.

"I'm so sorry it's taken me longer than expected to follow up," Jonah said sympathetically. "I've been really busy with other patients. I work with extended care patients and sometimes complications arise, you understand."

"I'm sorry to hear that," Anna stated sincerely. "Hope everyone is okay, or at least as okay as they can be depending on the situation."

"Thank you." Jonah paused. "Do you mind if I give you a quick checkup?" he asked with a smile.

"Oh, yea – sure," Anna replied. She followed his instructions as he examined her arms and legs for sores and fibers.

"Have you not been seeing many fibers show up?" he asked, not finding much. Anna smiled.

"No, I just can't stand them… I've been taking them out and putting them into little freezer bags with the dates on them. I thought that maybe you would want them for study," she added. "They're in the fridge."

Jonah smiled, and outside of Anna's view, so did James. Anna walked over to her fridge where she kept a shoebox with neatly arranged zippered plastic bags of fiber samples. Taking out several of them from various points in time, she set those back in her fridge, then brought the rest of them to Jonah. She didn't want to give them all away, especially if he was getting paid for them at her expense. She also thought that maybe it would still be possible to have them independently analyzed.

"I've kept them in chronological order, so hopefully that helps," she stated with a smile. Jonah nodded.

"It definitely does," he told her. "If we find anything useful, we'll let you know. These things can take time, though, so even with all the samples you're giving me, don't get your hopes up too high, okay?"

She frowned but nodded. "I understand," she said. "I'm going to continue to collect them that way so it's easier for everyone," she added and walked them both to the door.

"Thank you so much, Anna," Jonah said and shook her hand.

As Jonah turned and walked to the car, James smiled warmly at her. "It's good to see you," he said, giving her a half hug. Anna smiled.

"You too, James," she said.

The two men got into a black Lincoln with tinted windows and drove away as Anna closed her front door, suspicious thoughts racing through her mind. *They're probably going to sell those fiber samples and I won't hear from them for a while again....*

∞

Anna's eyes fluttered open to strange lights dancing all around her. She sat up and rubbed her eyes, hoping to see something tangible for once.

As she began to realize that she'd slept on the couch instead of in her bed, a hand clamped down over her mouth. She tried to scream but it came out as a muffled squeak. Her eyes shot open as she tried to see who her assailant was.

"*Shh*, Anna," a voice whispered urgently. She furrowed her brows. Why did that voice sound so familiar?

"I won't hurt you. You promise not to scream?"

Anna nodded her head.

The pressure on her mouth lightened. As the hand was removed, she was able to turn around to see who was in her house.

When she did, she had to bite her lip to keep from screaming.

"*Andrew?!*" she whispered. "You're supposed to be dead!" she said in disbelief.

"Supposed to, yes," Andrew said. "It's a ridiculously long story."

He pulled her up from the couch and embraced her, partially to prove he was real and partially just to feel some comfort, as fleeting as it may be. He wanted to forget everything that had happened to him while he was gone.

Anna relaxed in his arms and knew that he was definitely alive. "You have to tell me what happened," she said into his shirt.

"I will," he laughed. "But first, I want to show you this nifty little trick called locking your front door...."

Anna feigned offense and lightly tapped his arm, smiling.

"Alright, alright," she said, heading down the hall toward the entry. "I deserved that... I'll lock up."

"I'll boil some water for tea," he replied and headed toward the kitchen.

90

Chapter Eight

Andrew watched Anna as she made her way to various cupboards and drawers in the kitchen and prepared two cups of tea. She was humming a song he couldn't place and he just stared at her, enamored and finally feeling like he was allowed to show it.

"You okay?" she asked him. He just nodded and smiled.

They sat in silence, each wrapping their hands around their mugs and taking tentative sips of steaming chamomile.

"So, where have you been?" Anna asked. "The FBI came here to tell me you were dead," she added, feeling it was an important detail.

"The FBI?" he asked. He furrowed his brows and looked into his cup. "Why would that be the FBI's job?" he wondered.

"That's what I wondered," Anna replied.

"Well, I heard some pretty weird things while I was gone. They had me tied to a chair with a black bag over my head for a while, but I could still hear even if I couldn't see much," he said. "Something about their employers and the BQS, which I'd heard of before. I got the distinct feeling that their employers were definitely not what you would expect. There seemed to be several FBI agents there, too."

Anna was confused. "So... some weird organization kidnapped you and faked your death? But why?" She paused and studied him for a moment. "Is there something about you that I should know?" She squinted at him, somewhere between playful and cautious.

"That's just it," Andrew said, meeting her gaze. "I have no affiliations with the government. The only time I even had anything to do with the government was when I was selling them Morgellons fibers from Jody for the money. We thought they were doing research, but apparently that's not the whole story." Andrew chose his words carefully as he walked the line between telling the truth and lying.

Anna's eyes widened.

"Did anything similarly weird happen to you before? I mean... Wait a minute." She scrambled out of her seat to the kitchen cabinet where she'd stashed the box.

"Did you leave a box on my doorstep?" she asked.

Andrew looked down. "Guilty," he said. "I had a friend deliver it because I was still executing my escape plan."

Anna smiled. "Alright, so you're some kind of spy or

something, right? Executing your escape plan? No one talks like that." She laughed.

"Ugh, I know," he replied with a smile. "I've been around those suits for way too long. Now I sound like them; that's pretty sad."

"Okay, so how did you escape? And if that box was from you, who's Jody? And what are all of the medical charts about? And why do they want the fibers? And why is it important enough to tell me you're dead? I thought we were making progress... and why wouldn't they come after me, too? If it's the fibers that they want then why—" she stopped herself, took a deep breath, and exhaled slowly. "I don't understand everything in those files," she added, hoping she didn't sound too excited about this conspiracy idea. She just *knew* there was something else going on.

Andrew smiled as he inhaled deeply and sighed, amused by her enthusiasm.

"I'll start with that note in the box." He chugged the rest of his tea. "You don't happen to have anything stronger in the house, do you?" he asked. Anna nodded and got a fresh bottle of wine from the pantry.

"Jody," Andrew began, pausing to watch Anna fill the wine glasses. He took one of them and drank in long, slow gulps. Anna smiled and reached into a cabinet next to her to reveal a mostly full bottle of whiskey. Swirling its contents and then setting the bottle down on the table, she watched him fill his wine glass with the amber liquid.

"Jody was my fiancée several years ago," he finally said. "She had Morgellons, and it was strange how it started. There was no transition, no hint of oncoming illness, no signs to warn either one of us. When it showed up, it just showed up and that was it." He took a swig of his whiskey and set the glass down.

"So what happened?" Anna asked, taking a sip of wine from her glass and suddenly feeling the urge to get utterly and belligerently drunk, both out of relief and a need to forget. *This might be very bad,* she thought.

"She committed suicide," he said, a ghost of sadness passing over his face. "The note in the box is her suicide note. No one else knows about that note because it was just too weird to share. They need to find a new subject? Like she was being experimented on or something...?" He finished off his whiskey and poured more. Anna got up and brought him a tumbler and some ice.

"Is that what it was?" she asked him as she sat back down. "It must have been some pretty aggravating experimentation if she was that determined to make it stop."

Andrew just nodded. "Yea, she was pretty scared by what was happening to her. Then she started spouting conspiracy theories and I thought she'd lost her mind or was just trying to find some kind of justification for her illness that would make it bearable."

Anna finished her glass of wine and poured another, looking up just in time to see his eyes misting. He blinked a few times, downed the whiskey, and poured another.

"Part of the interest I had in Morgellons was inspired by her, simply because I saw all the symptoms of the disease. I saw how it changed her and I saw what was happening to her mental state because of it." He sighed. "I guess she could've handled it better, or maybe it just takes a longer time for it to affect others than it did her, but either way... she's gone, and I was never able to figure out exactly what happened."

"Is that why you were so interested in helping me?" she asked. Sipping on the glass of wine again, she waited for his reply, trying to remain objective about the conversation. She couldn't help but feel slightly uncomfortable and almost jealous because of the connection she'd always felt with him.

"At first, yea," he replied. "But that wasn't the only reason. I wondered if you had any of the mental symptoms that she had and if that was why you were admitted. I wanted to get to know you to see if there were similarities.

"It made me a little angry at first to know that you'd had this illness for months and didn't go crazy. For Jody it seemed like it came on so fast, like she was just going nuts right away."

"Okay, well what facts did you find when you did tests on her?"

"I found about the same things as I did with your tests. It seemed like the only difference was that she was more emotionally and mentally affected by it than you have been."

Anna looked down at her hands and felt a twinge of guilt.

"Well," she began, taking another sip of wine. "I would agree that it hasn't affected my emotional or mental state but that would be a lie," she said.

"How's that?"

"I've been having trouble sleeping," she stated. "Not that I can't fall asleep, though.... It's more like I can fall asleep fine and then at some point in the middle of the night, I wake up feeling like I was drugged and everything is blurry. Sometimes I feel like there are people in the room with me but I can never quite tell because I'm so out of it. Then there are pulling sensations... like someone is pulling on my arms and legs. Nothing ever happens — I mean I don't fall out of bed or anything — but it feels weird."

"And you're sure you're awake while this is happening?" he asked.

"As sure as I can be," she replied, taking another sip of wine. "I mean it's all so foggy that I'm never 100% sure, but it seems like I wouldn't remember it at all if I were asleep." She paused for a moment, then smiled. "You know those sleeps where you drift in and out of consciousness and start mixing reality with whatever world your subconscious has cooked up for you?"

"Yea, sure," he replied. "Is that what it's like?"

"Yea... except I don't remember it as a dream, I remember it like something that really happened. But dreams that seem real have that effect, too, I guess. The lines have never been *that* blurred for me before, though." She paused again. "And then some nights I wake up like something startled me and I can see moving shadows on my wall, even though there are no lights or anything. I'm usually wide awake when this happens, but by the time I go turn on the lights, there's never anything there. I feel like I'm being watched intently whenever this happens."

They sat in the kitchen in silence for a moment.

"Do you... want to move into the living room?" Anna asked. Andrew smiled and nodded, grabbing both bottles and his glass.

"I'd love to. After you," he said, motioning for her to lead the way.

"I don't know about you, but I have the urge to get really, really drunk." Anna wasn't sure why she said it out loud, but she felt like some dead-to-the-world sleep for 12 hours would do her a lot of good.

"I'm already on my way," he replied, holding up the bottle and pouring another glass. They sat down in the living room and continued their conversation, knowing that no real ground would be covered but taking comfort in each other's company.

As the evening progressed, they changed seats several times to either be more comfortable, be able to talk better, or be closer to whichever end table had their respective drinks. They laughed together throughout the night as the conversation flowed through various topics, and both felt as if they finally had a friend again. A real friend, someone who knew the depths of a shared cause... or obsession.

"So what are you going to do now?" Anna asked him suddenly.

"What do you mean?" he asked, his hand finding her knee. They progressively sat closer together as the night wore on and Anna was intensely aware of his touch. Coupled with a warm buzz, she felt like this might be an interesting night for them if he was feeling the same way.

"I mean, you can't go back to your house, right? Because you're dead." They both smiled.

"I honestly hadn't thought about it," he offered after a pause. "I knew that they'd harass you once I overheard what they were talking about... They had a weird obsession with the fibers, so I thought I should come talk to you. I didn't plan for much else," he added, smiling sheepishly.

"Oh," she replied. He gently stroked her knee with his thumb, and Anna did her best to maintain her composure. *Is this really happening?*

"Well, maybe I could sleep in your garage for a few days? I mean until I can figure out something more permanent...."

"And leave me in here by myself?" she asked. "To be perfectly honest with you, I would prefer if you stayed here more permanently.... especially now, knowing that there might be people after me. Or my fibers. Whatever."

"Are you sure?" he asked, removing his hand. Inside she protested, but outside she just nodded.

"Yea, of course I'm sure. I mean I'm a little buzzed and feeling like this may not be the best time to make any major life decisions, but I don't think this is a situation I can consult my friends on, you know?" She giggled a little.

He laughed. "I don't think that would be a very good idea," he agreed. His hand found her knee again and there was a moment of magnetic anticipation between them as their eyes met. Anna's lips parted slightly as her breath caught in her throat and Andrew grabbed her face and pulled her in for a deep kiss. Pent-up desires and wishful fantasies collided with relieved passion and drove them to fumble their way upstairs to her bedroom.

∞

Anna opened her eyes to bright sunlight. She stretched out and her arm touched Andrew's warm skin. She nearly jumped out of herself as she scrambled to turn toward him and gasped, realizing last night wasn't just some cruel dream. Presumed dead Andrew. Officially deceased Andrew. The-FBI-told-her-he-was-dead Andrew.

She lay there for a moment and took in the sight of him, his light olive skin smooth and soft, lying next to her in her bed. She looked at her own skin, riddled with sores and strange patterns forming beneath the top layers. She quickly covered herself with the sheet and cuddled up next to him.

"Good morning," Andrew said as he turned to her, his voice thick with sleep. He wrapped his arms around her and held tightly for a moment, Anna returning the gesture.

"We really—"

"Yep," he replied, not letting her finish. "And I'm perfectly happy about that," he added. "Are you okay?"

Anna nodded her head and maneuvered her body as close to him as she could.

"I'm okay," she said softly. He kissed her head and kept his arms wrapped around her, knowing exactly how confused and alone she probably felt. He couldn't even begin to imagine how alone she felt because of her condition, not to mention the fact that he'd disappeared for several weeks and she thought he was killed. *What a mess,* he thought.

He held her for a few moments, hoping she knew that he was sincere and serious about his feelings for her. Now that he didn't have to worry about being professional – he was officially dead, after all – he didn't feel as restricted in his interactions with her as he had before. He'd always felt connected to her... he just hadn't been able to do anything about it before without risking his career.

"When's the last time someone cooked you breakfast?" he asked with a smile. She twisted around to look at his beautiful face.

"I don't remember," she said with a grin.

Beaming his flawless smile at her, he jumped up and winked. "Today would be the right answer," he stated.

They spent the day poring over Andrew's research from the mystery box, sharing information, and one catching the other staring.

Anna took time to treat her skin with what she thought would help based on his suggestions. Overall, they had a wonderful day together.

Once dusk rolled around, they decided to put away the research and watch a movie to take their minds off of reality for a while.

Anna snuggled into Andrew's chest on the couch and, though it still seemed surreal that he was there, she allowed herself to feel comfort and contentment in his arms. They had a long road ahead of them to figure out what was going on with Morgellons, but there wasn't anyone else she would rather be working beside.

∞

"Oh my God, I almost forgot!" Anna exclaimed, jumping up from her cozy seat next to Andrew Sunday afternoon. They'd been lounging around, watching TV and playing around on the internet when she remembered her phone call with Casey the previous week. Had it really only been a week? She felt like a lifetime had passed with all of the information bombarding her mind and Andrew magically reappearing.

"What did you almost forget?" he asked curiously. He seemed equal parts concerned and amused, unsure of how to react.

"Casey invited me to dinner at her house," she said, smiling. "I can bring a date," she added, winking at Andrew as she gathered her socks and then jogged up the stairs to her bedroom to change.

"Oh?" he said to himself, eyebrows raised. "That sounds like fun," he said with a smile, following her upstairs to change.

"I feel like I've been neglecting her," Anna confided as she pulled on some jeans and a blouse. "She's always been an awesome friend, and here I am all involved in my own little world while she's raising three kids by herself," she added. "Not that she *needs* anyone," she added, heading into the bathroom to brush her teeth.

Andrew listened as he changed into his own more presentable clothes. She only stopped talking while she was brushing her teeth, and he thought that was amusing. *Anything to keep from being impolite*, he thought.

By the time she came out of the bathroom, she'd already washed her face and put makeup on, as well as sweeping her hair up messily into a clip. She was gorgeous.

"Are you ready?" she asked excitedly. "I don't know for sure what time she wanted us to be there, but she specifically said dinner on Sunday, so we're going." As if on cue, her cell phone rang. Anna grinned as she answered it.

"Hello?"

"Anna? Are you still coming over for dinner tonight?" Casey asked, sounding frazzled.

"I was just finishing getting ready. Am I early? Is it okay if I show up now?" She made it a point to make it sound like she would be coming alone.

"Aw, you're not bringing anyone? I invited Tom, but I don't want you to feel like a third wheel...." She trailed off. Anna giggled, wondering who Tom was.

"I'm bringing someone, don't worry," she said, hoping Casey wasn't too exhausted. "It sounds to me like you could use some help," she added, motioning to Andrew that they should leave.

"You know, I really could!" Casey cried, sounding exasperated. "I'm an awesome cook, but you'd never guess it with these three mongrels constantly cramping my style!" She laughed. "All they want is mac and cheese and hot dogs, I barely ever get to cook anything *real* and it's so sad!"

"Alright, honey. I'll be there to help with the munchkins shortly! Hang in there, because I really want to have some of your delicious cooking tonight." Anna beamed at Andrew as she hung up and they left the house for dinner.

She made sure she locked the front door.

∞

"I am so happy to see you!" Casey exclaimed as she opened the door to see Anna and Andrew. She threw her arms around Anna warmly, embracing her tightly. Then she gave Andrew a friendly hug and added, "It's nice to meet you! Both of you, come in, make yourselves at home!"

Anna and Andrew exchanged a warm smile and entered Casey's home. Her three young kids were chasing each other all over the house, running first through the hallway and then around the living room and kitchen.

"The kitchen is off-limits!" Casey yelled at the top of her lungs. "How many times do I have to say that?" she asked herself softly. She took a deep breath and exhaled slowly before turning back to her guests.

"Sorry about that. I love them to death, but they really get on my nerves sometimes," she said with a laugh. "I feel like a broken record most of the time, just repeating the same things every day and still not getting through. Isn't that the definition of insanity?" she added. They laughed. Casey and Andrew introduced themselves and shook hands.

"Well, let me wrangle these crazies!" Anna said playfully as she chased Casey's kids into the living room and they collapsed in a fit of giggles on the couch. "You know you're driving your mom nuts when she has very important work to do," she stated in a mock-serious tone.

Lisa suddenly became somber. "Important work?" she asked.

"Of course!" Anna exclaimed exaggeratedly. "She's cooking food for adults! Adults *never* joke about great food." Not quite sure what to make of that statement, Lisa sat quietly for a moment.

"So you don't like mac and cheese?" she asked, and Anna giggled.

"Don't you know you are what you eat?" she asked, maintaining her joking tone. "If you only eat mac and cheese, you'll turn into mac and cheese!"

Shocked and dismayed, Lisa shook her head in protest.

"You're a liar," Jason interjected, almost realizing that Anna was joking but still not completely certain.

"How do you *not* turn into mac and cheese?" Lisa asked. Anna thought for a moment.

"In order to keep your human form, you have to eat a balanced diet," Anna stated.

"What does that mean?"

"That means you have to eat a lot of different things to stay a healthy human," Anna explained. She giggled. "I'm just kidding, you guys. You won't turn into mac and cheese," she added, smiling. "How about some *eye* food?" Anna asked suddenly, changing the subject. Jason laughed.

"Eye food?" he asked. "What's *that*?"

"A movie, silly," Anna said with a smile and a wink. The kids nodded their heads in excitement and Anna went over to the TV to turn it on.

"Netflix!" All three of them said in unison. Anna chuckled.

"Casey, honey?" Anna said loudly toward the kitchen. "Is it okay if I put a movie on for the kiddos?"

"Please! *Anything* to hold their attention for longer than three seconds!" she replied. Anna smiled and shook her head.

"What do you think?"

Anna handled the debate about which movie to watch gracefully and chose one that she thought would keep their attention. Her son had been the same way, never sitting still. She'd developed an eye for choosing kids' movies with him and figured she could do the same for her best friend's kids... but more for her best friend so she could focus on the task at hand: working her magic in the kitchen.

The kids settled in for their movie, all of them contently snuggled up under a large blanket on the couch. And they were quiet. Anna beamed from ear to ear despite herself as she made her way to the kitchen to keep Casey and Andrew company. Tom hadn't arrived yet.

Anna made her appearance and Casey stopped for a moment.

"How the hell did you do that?" she asked softly. "I demand to know and you totally have to teach me that trick," she finished. Anna shrugged innocently, taking a seat next to Andrew at one of the counters where a glass of wine was waiting for her. Andrew smiled as she sat down, and he gave her a peck on the forehead.

"Aw, look at you!" Casey exclaimed with a warm smile. "How long has this scenario been playing out?" she asked. Anna and Andrew exchanged a glance.

"Not very long," Anna replied. "It's a pretty recent scenario," she added. As Casey turned back to her cooking, Anna touched Andrew's arm and mouthed, "Come here," so he would lean in close.

"What's up?" he whispered.

"I don't think we should talk about the specifics of anything that's going on tonight," Anna said softly. Andrew nodded his agreement. He'd already decided to let her take the lead on conversation topics.

"What are we talking about?" Casey said with her chin in her hands and her elbows on the counter right next to them and Anna jumped slightly.

"Jeez, Casey!" she said. Then she grinned and added, "Just some sweet nothings."

Casey laughed. "Alright, get a room, you two!" she joked and stood upright, taking a drink from her wine glass. Anna and Andrew just smiled.

"So, tell me a little bit about Tom," Anna said, curious about her friend's date.

"Well, it's nothing serious... yet," Casey began, swirling the wine in her glass around as she spoke. "I think this is our... third date, maybe? I learned a long time ago not to get my hopes up too fast," she added with a wink. Anna nodded knowingly and sincerely hoped that Tom would treat Casey well.

"How did you two meet?" Casey asked. She set down her glass and wandered over to the stove to check on the food briefly. Andrew looked to Anna to answer.

"You remember when I was held at the hospital for 72 hours?" Anna began. Casey gasped.

"Is this that doctor you told me about? The one who—" she stopped short and whispered. "The one who snagged your Morgellons sample or whatever and had his friend run tests on it under the radar?"

Anna smiled. "No, no... this is the friend," she stated. Casey's eyes widened and she grinned broadly.

"Dr. Mitchell told me about her case," Andrew said with a smile. "I have a kind of soft spot for Morgellons because I knew someone in the past who had it, and the condition has just always fascinated me, made me want to figure it out," he added.

"That is fantastic!" Casey said, her enthusiasm contagious. Anna still had no idea where her friend got the energy from. She felt drained just from her minor encounter with the kids, but at least they were happy and settled in for the time being. Anna knew that her disease was at least partially to blame for her lack of energy.

"Well," Casey added, "let me just say that you two make a beautiful couple and I hope for both of your sakes – and mine – that you get to the bottom of this mystery illness Anna has."

"Here's hoping!" Andrew said jovially and raised his wine glass. The three of them clinked glasses just as the doorbell rang.

"That must be Tom!" Casey exclaimed as she rushed to answer the door. Anna smiled, amused at Casey's quirky personality. Casey looked genuinely happy to see Tom, her green eyes sparkling as she walked to the door.

Anna had gotten up and partially followed Casey, hanging back to observe their greeting. She was suspicious of everyone these days, at least until she felt like she knew whom she was talking to.

As Casey opened the door and Tom entered and embraced her, Anna caught a glimpse of him and immediately recognized James.

Chapter Nine

"Anna, Andrew," Casey said, her green eyes bright. "I'd like you to meet Tom."

Anna watched as recognition flashed across his face, but she didn't see any surprise. There should have been surprise.

"Hi, Tom," Andrew said with a smile and a warm handshake, oblivious. "I'm Andrew, nice to meet you."

Anna stuck out her hand, knowing she needed to keep things subtle but feeling anger burning deep within her. How dare he mess with her best friend? And who the hell was he if he wasn't James?

"Nice to meet you, *Tom*," Anna said with a scowl masquerading as a smile. She watched as he flashed her a grin, comfortable with his lie to a disturbing degree. *Who the fuck does he think he is?* she wondered.

The four of them made their way back into the kitchen as Anna tried to maintain her composure. She excused herself to go to the bathroom and clear her head.

Patting her cheeks and forehead lightly with cool water, Anna stood and looked at her reflection. She was lucky the stupid Morgellons hadn't spread to her face... yet. Her face was still okay. She took several deep, cleansing breaths and tried to calm herself down.

Why in the world would someone give two different names? There was definitely more going on than she originally anticipated, and she couldn't wait to tell Andrew. Now that she was aware that James – Tom – whoever – was playing two different people, she had to play her cards right if she wanted Casey to stay safe. Her kids were a huge concern for Anna, and she couldn't imagine what kind of damage it would do to everyone if something bad happened.

Anna patted her face with a towel and took another deep breath, her thoughts collected. Her heart beat rapidly as she went back to the dining room to find dinner served and everyone sitting around the table congenially. She took her seat next to Andrew and across from Ja—Tom, smiling politely and doing her best not to let Casey see her distress. She made a mental note not to drink more than two glasses of wine. She needed to stay sharp, if for no other reason than to figure out what was really going on.

The conversation was already in full swing when Anna returned, so she just listened for a few minutes as she ate the smoked salmon dish her friend had prepared. For a moment, Anna was lost in the flavors. She didn't know how Casey pulled it off every time, but the meals she prepared were amazing. With hints of lemon and pepper colliding on Anna's tongue in beautiful harmony with the wine, asparagus, and artistically prepared sauce, Anna felt like her taste buds went to heaven for a brief moment.

Reality sent her poor taste buds crashing straight to hell as soon as she opened her eyes and saw Tom-James' face again, though.

"So, Tom, what do you do?" Andrew asked as they ate, keeping the conversation light. *Small talk definitely comes in handy sometimes,* Anna thought.

"I freelance, mostly," Fake Tom offered. "You know, construction, security, a little of this and that." He smiled at Anna as if taunting her. "What about you, Andrew?"

"Oh, I'm a doctor," he said. "On sabbatical right now, but you can never fully get away from your calling, am I right?" Tom offered a polite laugh in agreement.

"Absolutely," he said, then took another bite from his plate. "What about you, Anna?" He peered at her over his wine glass as he waited for her to answer.

"Oh, I freelance, too," she said, smiling. "A little of this and that," she added. Andrew could sense that she was being difficult on purpose.

"Casey?" Andrew asked, keeping the conversation flowing.

Casey smiled and let out a small laugh. "Considering I have three kids, the better question is what *don't* I do, is it not?" She winked at Anna playfully and Anna returned a smile. The four of them ate in silence for a moment, enjoying their food.

"Best vacation you've ever taken," Tom-James stated. "Anna?" He was picking on her, trying to get under her skin.

She didn't falter.

"The kind where people are who they say they are," she stated matter-of-factly, then chuckled like she was joking. "I've had some crazy experiences," she added. "Don't mind me!"

Andrew became uncomfortably aware of what was going on. Though Anna hadn't told him in detail about her new friend and his doctor buddy, he figured that Tom was probably one of them since Anna didn't have much of a social life. She avoided drama like a fish avoids dry land, yet it found her anyway. He wondered what Tom had to do with this weird situation.

"What about you, Casey?" Andrew asked, following the pattern of conversation. "What was your best vacation ever?"

Casey smiled broadly at Andrew and got a dreamy look in her eye. "Greece," she said. "The beaches are amazing... white sand and the bluest seas you've ever seen.... And that's all I'm going to say about that." The smile plastered on her face gave her away even as she tried to hide it by taking another bite of her food. Anna let out a little laugh despite her foul mood.

"Anna," Tom-James began again, and her smile faded quickly. "Are you feeling alright?" he asked. Anna shrugged.

"I'm fine, thanks," she said, furrowing her brows. *He must be messing with me,* she thought.

As if on cue, her vision began to blur and she felt dizzy. *I know I didn't drink that much,* she mused suspiciously as darkness closed in around her eyes. Within seconds, she fainted.

∞

By the time Anna woke up, several minutes had gone by and she felt wobbly as she stirred, like her consciousness was leaning on a rickety old table with uneven legs.

"Anna.... Are you okay?"

Anna's foggy brain managed to process Andrew's voice as she felt herself resurfacing. Propping herself up on her elbows, she realized that her entire chair had toppled over.

"What just happened?" she asked. Even in her foggy brain, she found it very strange that the only times she'd ever fainted like this were around James. Tom. Whoever he was. And what did he have to do with this whole Morgellons situation if he wasn't just an intern at the hospital? *Was* he even an intern at the hospital? She definitely felt like her suspicions were beginning to have merit.

Anna tried to lift herself from the ground and Andrew gently touched her arm.

"Take it easy for a minute," he said just as Casey handed him a glass of water with concern in her eyes.

"Is she okay?" Casey asked. "What happened? Has this happened before? Will she be alright?"

The kids had all fallen asleep on the couch to their movie, which Anna felt relieved about. She had no idea how they might handle a situation like this and felt it better that they just stayed ignorant to it.

Anna took the water and gulped down half the glass before motioning for Andrew to help her up from the floor.

"I'm okay," she said as she teetered for a second, getting her bearings and leaning on Andrew for support.

Tom-James was nowhere to be found.

Andrew held on to her elbow to steady her and gave Casey a sympathetic look.

"I'm so sorry," he offered. "I think I'd better drive her home so she can get some rest."

"Okay," Casey agreed and walked them to the front door. Giving Anna a hug, she added, "I hope you feel better soon, Anna."

"Sorry for ruining dinner," Anna offered weakly, and Casey shook her head.

"I think we were pretty much done, anyway," she replied with a concerned smile.

Andrew led Anna out to her car and she handed over the keys. The second he pulled out of the driveway, Anna began wondering out loud about her fainting spells.

"Both times I fainted Fake Tom was there," she stated.

"Who is he to you?" Andrew asked, eager to find out which guy he supposedly was.

"James. The one I met at the coffee shop who conveniently supposedly was an intern at the hospital and conveniently happened to find a doctor with an interest in Morgellons." She paused. "You know, according to the internet, which I know isn't fully reliable, but Morgellons only has about twenty thousand documented cases, putting the real count probably at forty or fifty thousand. That's still not common enough for two doctors in such close proximity to take an interest."

"I agree," Andrew offered. "Do you think that maybe he poisoned you or something?"

"Both times I drank wine, but only a glass, maybe two," she said, remembering the night James had brought Jonah to her house for dinner.

"Maybe he put something in your drink, then," Andrew said.

"Oh, God," Anna said suddenly, panic squeezing her heart. "We need to go back," she stated as she gave Andrew a severe look.

"What? Why?" he asked, furrowing his brows. "*You* need to get home and get some rest," he added.

"What about Casey and the kids?" she asked, raising her voice a little. "I couldn't forgive myself if that asshole did something to them!"

Andrew nodded, realizing what she meant.

"Okay. I understand," he said. "The house is only a few minutes away, so let me drop you off and then I'll go back to check on Casey and the kids to make sure. I'll say you forgot something or whatever."

Anna sat back in her seat, relief allowing her to relax a little.

"Okay," she said. "That sounds good." She closed her eyes and tried to imagine all of her questions away. She knew that would only come true once she found the answers, but her mind desperately needed some peace.

They got home and Anna immediately made her way to her bed, plopping down face-first and fully clothed.

Andrew smiled despite the somber mood that had taken over the night. Shaking his head, he sighed and pulled her into a sitting position on the bed gently.

"I don't want to come home to cuddle up to the outside of your jacket," he said softly as she stood and he began taking off her coat, his face just inches from hers. She smiled.

"Oh, I suppose I could accommodate," she replied. *Where did this man come from?* Her heart fluttered as he brushed his lips against hers gently and gave her a soft kiss before pushing her backward onto the bed. Her breath caught in her throat as she sat down, and at that point, she couldn't wait for him to get back.

Seeing the look in her eyes, he said, "Don't worry, babe. I just want to take your shoes off and tuck you in before I leave. I know you're concerned about Casey."

"Are you real?" she asked jokingly. "Most of the men I've been with would have said screw it, let's have a quickie.... I'm happy to know that you're a man of honor," she added, feeling herself falling in love with him.

"Hey, when I get back," he said, raising his eyebrows. "Just because I do what's right doesn't mean I won't come back and spoil you rotten," he said with a mischievous half-smile.

"Alright, get out of here," she said after he'd taken off her second shoe. "I'll be right here when you get back."

He gave her a kiss and left the bedroom, then headed back over to Casey's to make sure she and the kids were okay.

∞

As he pulled into Casey's driveway, nothing seemed different. He hoped to find Casey and the kids all safely inside, the kids in bed and Casey watching a movie or cleaning up after dinner. He didn't see any cars in the driveway except for Casey's, so he hoped that Tom or James or whoever he was had left.

Andrew knocked on the front door and waited for an answer. He'd only been gone about twenty minutes, so nothing too crazy could have happened... right?

Casey opened the door with a surprised smile.

"Andrew! Is everything okay?" she asked, motioning for him to come in.

"Yea, for the most part. Anna thought she might have forgotten her purse here, so I thought I'd come back and ask, maybe check for it," he said with a smile.

"How's she holding up?" Casey asked, her smile fading.

"I think she'll be fine," Andrew said, putting a comforting hand on her shoulder. "Are you okay?"

"Yea, I'm fine," Casey said. He followed her into the kitchen. "I don't know what happened to Tom. In all the commotion he just seemed to vanish and he didn't even bother to say goodbye. This is about the time I push him away and we cease our relationship, or whatever it is we have." She sighed and shook her head as she rinsed the dinner plates under hot water. "This happens to me *every time*, you know? I get involved and he turns out to be a sociopath... or a criminal. Or worse!"

Andrew wasn't sure what to say, but he sympathized. On an individual basis, he knew society was broken because people were broken. They broke each other, and it just caused more chaos and discord as a whole.

"Casey?" he said, prompting her to turn around to face him. She stood with a plate in one hand and a scrub brush in the other, dripping soapy water on the floor. He approached her and put the plate and the scrubber back in the sink, then squeezed her hands before letting go. She wasn't crying or anything, just... annoyed, like she'd repeated the same pattern way too many times.

"I think that you shouldn't worry about all that tonight," Andrew said. He had nothing in the way of relationship advice, but he certainly could tell that she was exhausted and stressed out. Nothing a good night's sleep wouldn't comfort.

Casey sighed heavily.

"You're right," she said. "I think I need to get some rest and look at this again tomorrow." She walked over to the counter where four nearly empty wine glasses stood. Before he could interject, Casey downed all four in rapid succession and sighed again, gathering the glasses to wash them.

Andrew wasn't sure how to react. If Tom had done something to one of the glasses, Casey would faint within minutes. If he hadn't, Casey was definitely not doing as well as she portrayed. Casey walked over to the sink and set the wine glasses on the counter next to it before reaching back into the water to keep washing dishes.

Andrew crossed the large kitchen and put a hand on her shoulder, gently turning her around and looking at her to check for possible signs up close. He furrowed his brows as he watched her pupils dilate.

"I feel weird," Casey muttered as her smile vanished and her eyes slid closed. Andrew managed to catch her and set her down on the floor gently, feeling that this was all the evidence he needed to confirm that Tom – James – had been poisoning Anna.

He wasn't after Casey. That was why he disappeared.

He was after Anna.

And Anna was home alone.

Chapter Ten

Andrew revived Casey and made sure she was okay before he left, but he left in a hurry. With a heavy knot growing in the pit of his stomach, he peeled out of Casey's driveway and took off, tires squealing.

Weaving through the sparse number of cars on the small town roads, he wished for a moment that he'd picked police officer instead of doctor as his career so he could get away with speeding like he was. Several people honked at him as he passed, but no flashing lights appeared in his rearview, so he kept going.

Once he got close to the house, he slowed down and kept only his parking lights on to pull into the driveway, shutting them off immediately after he put the car in park.

Adrenaline pumping, he opened the car door slowly and paused to listen for a moment before getting out and pressing the door shut quietly. He walked to the front door, tried the knob, and after realizing it was locked, he slowly unlocked the deadbolt and let himself in without turning on the lights.

The kitchen light was on, illuminating the living room enough so he could see a figure sitting on the couch. It definitely wasn't Anna.

"Glad you could make it," the man said calmly as he flipped on the lamp next to him.

"What are you doing here?" Andrew asked darkly. He kept his eyes on Tom-James but peripherally scanned the room for anything he could use as a weapon should it come to that.

"Calm down, I'm not here to hurt anyone," he stated, motioning for Andrew to take a seat. Andrew cautiously obliged.

"What do you want?" he asked. "No, you know what? Let's start with what your name actually *is*." Andrew's heart was still racing but he tried to calm down without letting his guard down.

"My name is James. The Tom thing was just to make contact."

"Make contact? What do you mean?" Andrew's brain moved from anger to intrigue.

"You," James began, "are supposed to be dead."

Andrew didn't respond.

"At least to Anna you're supposed to be dead," James continued. "To my employers at the BQS, you're supposed to be working on something."

"I told them I didn't want to," Andrew stated. James smiled.

"Ah, but what you want doesn't matter anymore, especially where Anna is concerned."

Andrew stood defensively.

"Don't bring her into this," he said with his fists clenched.

"Andrew... you may not realize this now, but Anna is an important piece to a very large puzzle, and the part she has to play doesn't involve you."

"And she doesn't get a say in this whole mess?" Andrew countered.

"Fate decided who would participate, nothing else. She was just one of many chosen by fate."

Confused, Andrew sat back down.

"You're not making any sense. Why do you keep drugging her to make her faint? Casey drank that wine, too, you know. She fainted when I went to go check on her to make sure she was okay."

James furrowed his brows. "Why wouldn't she be okay? I have no interest in her. My interest is in you and why you're not doing what you were assigned when we let you go."

Andrew sighed heavily and lowered his head.

"I don't want to lie to her."

"So... if you just don't do it, you have nothing to hide... but if you do, you have to lie to Anna? Am I getting this right?"

Andrew nodded.

James raised his voice just enough and said through clenched teeth, "You realize that by *not* cooperating with us you're putting her life in danger, don't you? You'd rather see her dead than lie to her?"

Andrew's eyes widened at the threat and James straightened up in his seat as he watched his message sink in. Unsure of what to say, Andrew sat back, feigning defeat while running scenarios in his mind in search for a solution.

"Now that we're on the same page, can we agree to disagree but still manage to accomplish the mission?"

Andrew nodded numbly. He didn't know what else to do. These people were powerful... not part of the government, but a corporation with private funding backing them who worked alongside the government. He knew he couldn't win by arguing with James or the BQS.

"Knowing what you know now, are you prepared to get back to your assignment? Which, coincidentally, will be much easier since you decided to let Anna know you're alive. Not the plan, but it's working out for the best anyway. Just don't let anyone else see you or the whole thing will be blown."

Andrew nodded. He kept his expression blank, but inside he was fuming... and determined, a dangerous combination. He would find a way to save Anna from whatever these people were trying to do to her. He had to. He was also determined to learn what was really going on.

James stood and put out his hand to shake Andrew's. Andrew just stared at it, looking at James with smoldering eyes.

"We're done here then," James said. He walked out the front door like nothing had happened, leaving Andrew to brood alone.

∞

"When did you get back last night?" Anna asked the next morning as she propped herself up and looked at Andrew.

"It was pretty late," he told her, tucking a stray strand of hair behind her ear as he smiled. "You were dead to the world," he added with a grin.

"Aw, and I was so looking forward to being spoiled," she grinned. "Coffee?"

"Definitely," he said. They made their way into their robes and down the stairs to the kitchen where Anna started a pot of coffee.

"So what happened?" she asked after noticing him staring absently.

"Huh?"

"At Casey's, goof," she said with a chuckle. "Obviously nothing too crazy, otherwise you would remember."

"Oh, Casey's perfectly fine. She and the kids aren't in any danger," Andrew said as he put his arm around Anna, pulling her into a hug. "I think she has some man issues to work out, though. She doesn't seem to think she has very good luck with dating."

Anna sighed. "Yea... more often than not, something bad comes out about the guy. Criminal history, mental health stuff, all kinds of craziness. It usually ends up being something really terrible to where she feels like he can't be trusted around the kids, you know?" Anna shook her head. "It's too bad, too. She could really use someone in her corner, you know what I mean?"

Andrew nodded. "Yea... I know what you mean."

"So nothing bad or weird happened?" Anna asked. Andrew shook his head no. "Alright, well that's at least something," she said, grabbing two coffee mugs out of the cabinet. "Are you okay?"

"Huh? Yea... I'm fine, babe," Andrew said with a big smile. He was still trying to figure out how he could tell Anna what he was involved in while making sure no one from the BQS or the FBI hurt her... or worse.

"Alright," Anna smiled back. "Don't you go all weird on me now, too," she half-joked.

∞

There's something bothering him and he isn't telling me, Anna thought as she peered over her coffee mug at Andrew. She knew she was falling in love with him. But she also knew that she could never be with someone who wasn't open with her. That had the potential to turn into her relationship with her ex-husband after Ezra died all over again, and she wasn't sure if she could bear that. Ezra's death had been bad enough, but instead of working through their grief together, Nolan had completely shut down and ended up having an affair and then leaving her all together.

With a sigh, she dismissed the painful memories and sat at her laptop to play a few rounds of Solitaire. If he wanted to tell her, he would. Maybe it was something difficult. Then again, maybe something *had* happened at Casey's and he didn't know how to tell her.

Anna decided to let it go for the time being and just concentrate on trying to figure out her disease. There was way too much going on to ignore, and the only way to find answers was to delve deeper. So she did.

"I wonder if you could maybe do some independent testing on these fibers," Anna murmured as she re-read her medical file for the umpteenth time. Focusing fully on Andrew, she continued, "I mean... there has to be something we're missing, right? Something to connect all the strangeness...." Her eyes widened. "I bet Tom or James or whatever knows way more than he's letting on. At dinner he was totally toying with me. And that fainting thing... he must be in pretty deep if he's comfortable with all the lying and slipping poison into my drinks. Don't you think?"

Andrew didn't look up.

"Andrew?"

"Huh?" He looked up in surprise. Anna sighed.

"I was asking if there was any way you could do some independent testing on the fibers," she said softly, shaking her head. It bothered her that she knew something was wrong but he wouldn't tell her. In fact, she had the sneaking suspicion that he *knew* she knew, but he still chose not to open up. She found herself getting angry at the situation.

"I'm so sorry," he said, taking her hand. "Look... I'm just really preoccupied with all this and I want to get it figured out, okay?"

Anna shot him a skeptical look but sighed.

"Fine," she said. "I'd really like you to tell me what's going on with you," she added, annoyed and pushing down feelings of abandonment that echoed from her past. "I don't want to repeat what happened to my marriage, you know? I don't know if I could take that." She got up and walked away in frustration, leaving her coffee and medical record on the table. "I'm going for a walk, clear my head. I hope you're more... available when I get back."

She grabbed her jacket and walked out the front door trying not to let her emotions get to her. She knew that she might be overreacting, but she also knew there was something going on. She couldn't get a grasp on what, though, which drove her nuts, especially with her intuition being set off like this and her thoughts going wild with speculation. Her instincts had always been good, usually with staggering accuracy. Why couldn't she figure out what Andrew was up to?

Anna didn't know what to make of anything anymore. She had no idea who she could trust if she couldn't trust Andrew. She could trust Casey, but Casey had so much on her plate.... Anna really wasn't fond of adding more burden to Casey's life, especially after the whole Tom incident.

Casey was reasonable enough, but she had her moments. There were times Anna had witnessed her lack of ability to handle stress, and she knew the small things always piled up to form one giant thing. There was no way she could do that to her friend, especially not when it came to something as big as all of the weirdness surrounding

Morgellons. Although... Anna knew full well that her friend would be fascinated with a mysterious potential conspiracy.

Anna sighed and took a deep breath of fresh air. She pretended to exhale all of her thoughts a few times and focused on putting one foot in front of the other.

∞

Andrew put his hand on his forehead in frustration.

"Why do you insist on letting this crap come between you and Anna?" he asked himself aloud, shaking his head.

He decided he had to make it up to her, if not tell her everything. They'd spent the day poring over paperwork and searching for clues – anything they had missed or skipped over. It was mid-afternoon now, almost dinner time, so he got up and put everything back into the box and started washing some dishes.

He felt guilty because they'd never ventured too deeply into her past in conversation, so he was surprised when she brought up her ex-husband. He also wondered what had happened, but he knew it couldn't have been good judging by her reaction. Being distant or preoccupied must have played a role, otherwise she wouldn't have reacted the way she did, as minor as her overreaction had been.

Andrew decided to make her dinner. He couldn't cook a lot of different dishes, but he made some pretty good pasta, so he decided to make her Fettuccine Alfredo with chicken and broccoli.

As he put the water on to boil, he wished that there was someone he could talk to about his situation. They didn't even want him to do anything horrible to her, just monitor her progress, although he wasn't sure what that entailed. He wouldn't know until it happened. All he was told was to send in progress reports every week after monitoring her Morgellons and any other health-related things that he noticed.

"If she has the fucking sniffles, you write it down and include it in your report, understand?"

Andrew sighed, shaking off the memories. As he put the noodles in the boiling water, the house phone rang. For a moment he wasn't sure if he should answer or let the machine get it, considering his status. He decided to wait for the machine to be sure.

Beep!

A woman cleared her throat, then said, "Hi there.... Um, this is going to sound a little strange, but I work at Deeplake Market and Anna's here. She... um... can't remember how to get home." A nervous chuckle. "I know, it sounds crazy, but she's right here, kind of looking a little—"

"Hello?" Andrew picked up the receiver.

"Hello?"

"Yea, hi... I'm Anna's boyfriend," he said. "You said she's at the grocery store?" he asked.

"Um... yea," the woman answered.

"Well, thank God for living in a small town, right?" he said, trying to keep his stomach from dropping to the floor. *Can't remember her way home?*

"Yes," the woman said. "I suppose. Is she okay?"

"You know," Andrew said, reaching into his mind for a good explanation. "She's been a bit sick lately, some kind of rare illness, so this might have something to do with that." He let out a nervous laugh. "I'll be there in a few minutes to get her."

"Okay...."

He hung up the phone and rushed out as he grabbed the car keys. Pulling into the store parking lot a few minutes later, he got out quickly and jogged inside, hoping Anna was alright. As he entered, Anna saw him from one of the checkout counters and her face lit up.

"Andrew!" she said, rushing to him and giving him a hug.

"Are you okay?" he asked her after a moment. "She said you couldn't remember how to get home... is that true?"

"You know," Anna started, "I got here, and I decided to stay and pick up a few things before heading home. Then I paid, and I walked outside and just didn't know which way to go. I don't know what happened," she said, looking concerned but almost comfortable, like this had happened before.

Andrew embraced her again.

"Well, where are the groceries you bought?" he asked. The woman at the check stand gestured to a bag of groceries still sitting on her counter and shot Andrew a confused look. He grabbed the bag and ushered Anna to the car, hoping his noodles weren't boiling over at home.

He didn't know what to make of this. Was it a new symptom or something else entirely?

As he got into the driver's seat, she smiled at him. "Hi," she said sweetly, leaning over to give him a kiss. *Did she forget about our almost-argument, too?*

He got her back home and a lightbulb seemed to go off as she stepped out of the car and walked to the front door.

"Oh my God, I can't believe I forgot *that!*" she stated. "How embarrassing," she mumbled.

"Are you sure you're okay?" Andrew asked as he opened the front door with one hand and juggled the grocery bag with the other.

"Yea," she said with a dismissive wave. "I'm better now that we're home.... *Mmm*, something smells great!"

Andrew shut the front door and followed Anna into the kitchen where the noodles were boiling and the chicken and sauce smelled wonderful. He'd chopped the broccoli into fine enough pieces to add them to the sauce and it looked like the whole meal was almost done even though he'd left the house for a few minutes. *Disaster averted,* he thought.

He couldn't make sense of how calm Anna was. It was like she wasn't completely herself... or like she was undergoing some kind of change that affected her mind. That couldn't possibly be a good thing.

"Anna?" he said gently as he pulled out a chair for her to sit down in.

"What's up?" she asked, smiling.

"When's the last time you let me take a look at your skin for new fibers?" he asked.

"Um," she thought for a moment. "I think it was last week, actually. We should probably do that soon, huh?"

"Yea...." He turned away to prepare a plate for each of them and furrowed his brows.

What the fuck is going on?

Chapter Eleven

As Anna and Andrew relaxed on the couch that evening, Anna thought about what she should teach Sophia at their art lesson the next day. She knew Sophia loved the watercolor and salt technique, but she wanted to focus on something strictly paint again. Before too long, Anna realized that they'd never even touched on the subject of texture, so she decided that was what she would teach her.

"I take it you decided what to teach Sophia tomorrow?" Andrew asked with a smile as she set down her laptop on the coffee table.

"Yep," she replied with a grin. "We're going to learn all about texturing, which I think Sophia will love."

"Good! I'm glad you figured that out," Andrew replied. He could tell that Anna was excited about seeing Sophia again, which made him happy despite his worry. "How are you doing otherwise?" he asked, wrapping his arm around her as she leaned against him on the couch.

"I'm okay," she said. "I've been thinking a lot about how I reacted earlier and I feel like I owe you an apology," she added.

"It really wasn't that bad," Andrew said, but Anna continued.

"I like to think I'm a fairly reasonable person," Anna said, taking on a serious tone. "But I have been feeling really strange some days... kind of like I'm not quite myself," she added. Andrew furrowed his brows.

"Do you think it has something to do with your sickness?" he asked.

"I don't know," she said, shrugging her shoulders. "If it does, that's kind of scary... I mean, what if I have fibers in my brain?" she asked. Andrew's eyes widened as his thoughts raced through the implications of that concept. After a brief moment, she shuddered and continued. "I wanted to talk to you about something, though. Maybe... maybe it'll help you understand me better when I do have weird moments, know what I mean?"

"Of course," Andrew replied. "You can tell me anything," he added.

"Well... I was thinking that I know a lot about your past just from what I've read and what we talked about concerning Jody and Morgellons. But you hardly know anything about my past because our focus has been so dedicated to this disease that it just never came up." Anna sat up and maneuvered to sit facing him on the couch. He took her hands into his own and smiled warmly.

"Don't feel pressured into telling me anything you don't want to because of a minor incident, Anna," he said, and she returned his smile.

"Oh, no," she said. "That's not it. I just think it's important for you to know a couple of things about what happened so that you know what's going on behind the scenes if I act weird." She hesitated for a moment and looked down, dread in the pit of her stomach at the next thought she would voice. "If... if this illness does affect my mind, you might need to know some of this stuff, too," she added. Andrew shared in her sinking feeling at the prospect, but stayed quiet so that she could say what she needed to say.

"About six years ago, my son died," she began. Andrew squeezed her hands gently and watched her face as she spoke. "His name was Ezra. He was almost eight and was on his way home from a soccer game in a carpool driven by one of the other moms." A tear fell from her right eye and Andrew's heart went out to her. He wanted to embrace her, but knew that she needed to get what she wanted to share with him out before he did anything.

"It was evening, about eight o'clock, and... and the van got hit by... by a drunk driver," she said, wiping her tears with her finger and taking a deep breath. "So then, my ex and I started having problems," she said, her expression and tone moving away from sadness toward resentment and anger.

"Nolan was a lot different from me when it came to grieving," she continued. "He pretended everything was fine for a while, but he got very angry. I basically drowned myself in wine for a few months. Once I sobered up and finally dealt with the loss – or at least tried to – he was beyond anger and just shut down emotionally all together. Eventually it got to the point where it felt like I was all alone, dealing with this loss, and he seemed perfectly fine but became a stranger to me. It was like we were roommates, politely living in the same house but not talking about anything important and no longer having any kind of intimacy to speak of."

Andrew started putting the pieces together and realized why she'd been so hurt by his lack of sharing. If he'd known about this before, he might have made it a point to make sure he wasn't so lost in thought.

"Long story short... I think part of him blamed me for Ezra's death because I was supposed to be driving that night and ended up calling one of the other moms to do it. I can't even remember why... it was so stupid. I also think that he felt like he couldn't talk to me because I was dealing with my own grief, and he didn't want me to take on his, too. Anyway, eventually he started having an affair, so on top of us not communicating and him being distant, he found comfort elsewhere and abandoned me when I needed him the most." Anna didn't shed any tears as she said this. It was almost as if she had never fully gotten over it.

"Anna?" Andrew said, gently using his fingers to lift her face so she could see him. "None of that was your fault," he said. "None of that was your decision, either. Your ex made his choice, and he forgot that he vowed to choose you every day for the rest of his life." Anna smiled as a tear fell and found herself falling even more in love with Andrew.

"I know it's probably hard for you to completely trust anyone," he continued. "But just know that I'm here for you now, and that I am choosing you every day because I'm falling more in love with you all the time," he said sincerely. Anna launched herself toward him and wrapped her arms around him tightly. He embraced her and kissed her head, hoping that she felt better now that he knew about some of her issues. Dredging up those old memories couldn't have been easy for her.

"Thank you," Anna said with a smile as she pulled away. "I'm glad you're you," she added, and they both laughed.

"On that note," Andrew said after a pause, "it's getting late. What do you think? Should we head to bed?"

"Yea," Anna replied. They stood and held hands as they made their way up the stairs, relieved after their heart-to-heart.

"I think maybe I should check your skin before we settle in completely. Sound good?" he asked. She just nodded and wore a big, cheesy, contagious smile. Andrew chuckled and smiled back at her, completely enamored.

∞

Anna found herself drifting along in a numb haze again, her body feeling light as a feather and her mind foggy. The silhouettes didn't surprise her anymore, but they still made her feel uneasy. And why did the shadows never have faces?

She felt the tugging sensations again and almost took comfort in the familiarity of it all. There was a bright light above her and the shadows were moving slightly, like they were working on her somehow.

As the numbness faded into darkness, she found herself slowly waking up, surfacing from the unconscious world to reality. As she opened her eyes, all she saw was darkness...

... and two dim, red eyes staring into hers. She couldn't move, and that was when fear gripped her.

"You're not real," she whispered. The red grew brighter for a moment, then faded again, as if the shadow was responding to what she said. Finally, she squeezed her eyes shut. "It's not real," she muttered to herself over and over, afraid to look. Part of her knew that it was real, and she could feel it staring down at her just inches away, floating above her like a ghost.

"Anna?" Andrew's voice sounded far away. "Anna, are you okay?" he asked.

Reluctantly, she opened her eyes. When she did, she still saw the red eyes gazing down at her... watching her.

It was still there!

Unsure of what else to do, she let out a terrified scream.

∞

"Are you sure you're okay?" Andrew asked a little while after calming her down.

"I'll be fine," she said, trying to convince herself as much as him. "It was just another stupid nightmare...."

"Anna, you were screaming like something scared the hell out of you," Andrew said, concern etched on his face.

"I know... it was scary," she said, cuddling up as close as she could next to Andrew.

"What in the world were you dreaming about?" he asked, hoping that talking about it would help her relax.

"I don't want to talk about it right now," she said softly. "Will you please just hold me? I need you to hold me...."

As he did, they both drifted back to sleep for several more hours until her alarm went off, Anna trying to forget the crippling fear and Andrew wondering what her dreams could possibly be about.

∞

At 10:00 AM, Dr. Schwartz dropped Sophia off at Anna's house for her art lesson. As soon as Anna opened the door to let her in, she noticed that Sophia seemed sad.

"Aw, Sophia... what's wrong?" Anna asked her. Sophia came in and gave Anna a hug, clinging to her waist tightly.

"I miss my mom," she said, her voice muffled by Anna's shirt. Anna stroked her hair gently and nodded.

"I know, little one. I'll bet your mom misses you, too," she said. "Any particular reason this is affecting you so much today?"

"It's her birthday," Sophia said softly, lost in memories. "Dad used to take me and Mom out to dinner, but... we haven't done that since...."

Anna led Sophia to the couch where she had her sit down and took a seat next to her. Little Sophia was still grieving the loss of her mother, just like Anna had some days when the loss of her son hit her like a semi-truck.

Anna touched Sophia's face, the little girl's blue eyes closed as a stray tear rolled down her cheek.

"I know it hurts, honey," Anna said, unsure of what the right thing to say was. They had both experienced loss, but Anna knew that the grieving process was different for everyone, and she couldn't begin to imagine how a child would handle losing her mother.

"I just wish I could talk to her, you know?" Sophia said, another tear making its way down her cheek. "I really miss my mom and having another girl in the house," she added with a little smile. Anna smiled back warmly.

"Well, I know it isn't the same, but you can talk to me if you need to," she offered. "I'm here to help, okay?"

Sophia nodded, gave Anna another big hug, then dried her tears.

"What are we going to paint today?" she asked. The moment had passed for Sophia, but Anna's heart went out to her. She wondered if Dr. Schwartz had dated anyone after Sophia's mother passed away....

It was probably too soon for him. As children, time seems to move slowly, but as adults, time flies by with the chaos of everyday life and responsibilities.

"I was thinking I would teach you about texturing with acrylic paints today," Anna said with a smile. Something was still nagging at her. "Are you okay now, honey?"

"I'm okay, Anna," Sophia replied, squeezing Anna's hand. "I just really miss my mom sometimes and my dad is always busy working, so... I don't really have anybody to talk to about anything except when I come over to your house," Sophia went on.

"How well do you remember your mom?" Anna asked, curious. Sophia smiled.

"I remember everything," Sophia said, her eyes lighting up. "She was so beautiful and had the warmest hugs and the softest hands.... She always let me brush her hair even if I wasn't good at it," Sophia said, laughing. Anna smiled.

"It sounds like you and your mom have some excellent, happy memories together," Anna remarked. "It's important to remember the good things more than the bad things," she added. Sophia nodded.

"I don't feel as sad when I remember the happy things," she said. Anna stood up and offered Sophia a hand.

"Well, good," Anna said. "Let's keep it that way and try to stay focused on the happy things today, too, okay?" she asked. Sophia nodded and stood, then followed Anna upstairs to the sun room to paint.

∞

Later that night, Anna found herself absent-mindedly rubbing her arms and trying not to accidentally catch any of the scabs that seemed to have become a permanent fixture on her body. Andrew sat next to her, engrossed in the show they'd decided on.

Suddenly, Anna stopped and pulled up her sleeve.

"You just checked my skin last night," she stated to Andrew, who nodded.

"Yea... I did," he said, furrowing his eyebrows. "What's up?" he asked.

"Do you happen to remember where the wounds were when you did that?"

"Some of them," he replied. "Why? What's going on?" he asked, moving closer to inspect her arms and legs.

"I could've sworn there was one right here yesterday," she said, indicating a spot on her left arm.

"And you had another dream last night..." Andrew added. "I do remember you having a spot there...."

"But last night's dream was scary... a lot scarier than the first one where a couple of the wounds disappeared," Anna said, unsure whether she should be relieved or filled with dread. The dreams seemed to be getting worse, and so was her condition... and neither she nor Andrew had any idea how a wound could vanish overnight.

Andrew wrapped his arms around her.

"We'll figure this out," he whispered, sympathizing with how she must've been feeling.

"I hope so," she replied, still feeling disturbed by the entire scenario. Did the dreams induce super-fast healing powers or something? If so, how? And why? And did that mean the shadow creatures truly did exist?

What in the world is happening to me?

Chapter Twelve

Because of Anna's nightmares, Andrew had decided it was best to do as he was told and write everything down in a stupid weekly report. Anna had seemed fine again, all things considered, and remembered everything later, which frustrated her a little bit because she was now feeling like she couldn't even trust her own mind. She still suspected that he was hiding something, but he had vowed to make sure he paid more attention to her and stopped wandering around in la-la land.

He just couldn't shake the nagging feeling that he should tell her the truth, though. The only thing holding him back was the thought that telling her might put her in more danger. He couldn't have that.

"I think I'm going to meet Casey for a cup of coffee," Anna said as she grabbed her coat and car keys from the entry. "I won't be too long, maybe an hour or two," she said with a smile. Andrew walked to the entry to give her a goodbye kiss.

"Are you feeling okay?" he asked. She looked fine, but she'd looked fine when she left for that walk, too, except for being annoyed with him.

"I'm fine, baby," she said, kissing him on the lips. "I've gotten some rest, plus I haven't seen her since our failed dinner. I want to make sure she's okay."

"Alright. But call me if you need anything," he said as she left the house. *As if I could do anything for her without a car,* he thought. "I hope she doesn't need anything," he muttered to himself.

His cell phone vibrated in his pocket. As he took it out, he looked at the caller ID and saw a number consisting of only zeros. *Weird,* he thought. He picked up and heard James' voice on the line.

"I assume you decided to do your job and write a report on her progress?" he asked. Now that Andrew knew he was employed by the BQS, James didn't even bother covering up his calculated tone anymore. This man seemed completely heartless.

"Yes, I have a few things to share," Andrew stated.

"Good! I'm going to give you an address. It isn't far, so you should be able to deliver it by tonight... say, by 9:00 PM? Any time you find about 15 minutes to spare and run your notes over there is fine.

There's a mail slot, hard to miss. Just slip your findings in there and you're all set."

"Okay," Andrew said, dreading the idea of making excuses to run some mystery errand.

"*Andy*," James said mockingly. "Don't worry so much about Anna. You won't have to lie to her forever."

Click.

Andrew looked at the receiver in confusion. *What's* that *supposed to mean?*

Realizing he only had one copy of his notes, Andrew decided to make an extra copy with Anna's three in one printer. Once he finished, he shoved the originals into an envelope and sealed it. He'd written the address down on a sticky note so he wouldn't have to memorize it and mentally prepared himself to go to this mystery location and drop off his notes. He needed to figure out what to tell Anna so she wouldn't be suspicious.

He felt *wrong* about the whole thing.

Before he could wallow in his stew of emotions, the front door flew open and Anna stalked in angrily.

"What's wrong?" Andrew asked, baffled.

"Really?" she asked. "*Really?!* I know now why you've been acting so weird!" she said loudly.

"What do you mean?" He had no idea what she was talking about.

"When were you gonna tell me that Casey fucking fainted while you were over there?! And what else is going on that would make you forget something as important as that?"

Andrew's heart sank. Had he really forgotten to tell her that? *Moron!*

"I'm sorry," he said, raising his hands in surrender. Anna just glared at him, her hurt buried somewhere beneath her anger.

"She's my *best friend*, Andrew," Anna emphasized. "How could you not tell me that? Not just because I was worried about her, but also because it proves that James or Tom or whoever the fuck he is was behind my mystery fainting episodes!"

"I know," Andrew said, lowering his head. "I'm so sorry, Anna." How could that, of all things, have slipped his mind? "I guess I got caught up in what she said before she fainted, especially since I made sure she was okay before I left...."

Anna just shook her head, sighed, and went upstairs, closing one of the doors firmly.

"Fuck."

∞

Anna ran a bath and tried to calm down, which seemed more difficult than usual. She didn't want to be mad at Andrew, but the way he was acting was driving her nuts. Her absolute, number one pet peeve – the worst thing someone could *ever* do to her – was lie, even if it was a lie of omission. She despised secrets, and she knew in her gut that something was going on that she wasn't privy to. She also knew that the nagging feeling in the pit of her stomach wouldn't go away until he told her everything, which made her emotionally and physically uncomfortable.

She distracted herself by lighting a few candles and taking a bath. Part of her wanted to get a glass of wine, but she didn't want to go back downstairs so she slipped out of her clothes and into the tub.

A few minutes later, there was a soft knock at the bathroom door.

"Anna?" Andrew said.

"Hm?" Anna replied, much calmer now.

"I brought you something," he said and opened the door. She sat up as he came in with a glass of wine, and she couldn't help but smile, completely disarmed.

"Wow," she said. "I thought about grabbing a glass but didn't want to go back downstairs.... Thank you." She accepted his peace offering and didn't protest when he sat down on the toilet cover to talk to her.

"Listen... I'm really sorry I didn't tell you about Casey."

"I know," Anna said.

"Can we go back to being us now?" Andrew asked with a hopeful smile. Anna let out a short laugh.

"We were never *not* us!" A somber look crossed her face. "You know I hate secrets."

Andrew nodded.

"You know that if anything is going on you can tell me, right?"

He nodded again.

"If there's anything else, will you tell me?" she asked. Andrew sighed.

"There is," he said. "I think I need to tell you now so that it can't hang over our heads later, because I feel like if we don't stand together, we won't make it."

"What do you mean?" Anna asked.

"I think you're right about there being something bigger going on," he began. "The night of the dinner.... I came home and James was sitting on the couch in the dark, waiting for me."

"What?! He was in my house?!"

Andrew touched her hand gently. "Let me finish," he pleaded softly. Anna sat back and gestured for him to continue.

"He was waiting for me because when I was gone, the BQS gave me a sort of... assignment. Like a long-term mission, I guess. James – not Tom – was here because he was sent to check up on me since I haven't been doing what they said. I thought I could just avoid it and maybe it would go away, but these people are serious... and dangerous."

"Dangerous?"

"He said that if I didn't comply with what they wanted, you would be in danger. I assume that means they'd send someone to kill you... or worse. And I wasn't supposed to tell you anything, either, but that has been really difficult."

Anna's jaw dropped. "This is way bigger than I originally thought, then," she stated, shocked. Andrew nodded solemnly.

Anna finished the rest of her wine, handed Andrew the glass, and climbed out of the tub.

"Enough relaxing then," she said. "We need to figure this out, so we should brainstorm how to analyze the fibers. You worked in a lab, right?"

Anna got dressed as she spoke, her mind racing.

"If James knew who you are, he inserted himself into my life on purpose. He deliberately found me, and then he deliberately fucked with Casey and her kids to get your attention, and maybe mine, too. We need to know more," she finished.

Andrew was amazed by her need for the truth as well as her determination to get it despite being sick.

"I love you...." The words escaped his lips before he could think about what he was saying.

"I love you, too," she replied with a bright smile and adjusted her hoodie a final time. "Let's go; we won't find answers without the fibers, and to analyze them, we need equipment."

She took his hand and pulled him downstairs to the kitchen where she opened the fridge and found her shoebox of samples. Unbeknownst to Andrew, she'd been keeping up on her Morgellons well, taking viable samples from her sores and storing them in zippered baggies in the fridge.

"You've been doing this on your own the whole time?" he asked. Anna looked at him and smiled.

"The last time someone came to collect these stupid things was when James brought Jonah here for some quick cash. They haven't been back because Jonah doesn't actually give a shit about the fibers or Morgellons, just the money. I saved them anyway." Anna winked at him and grabbed the whole box but put a handful of baggies back into the fridge. "Just in case," she said.

"In case what?" he asked, dreading the worst.

"Anything," she said simply.

They left the house hurriedly at 2:00 PM.

∞

"Hi there," Anna said, smiling at the library desk clerk. "I was wondering if we could use the computers, just for a few hours?"

"You need a library card for that," the chubby man behind the desk stated and pointed at a stack of forms. "It's easy... one page. Just fill them out."

"We're on a road trip," Anna said enthusiastically. "I doubt we'll ever be back since we came all the way from Maine, but I have to check my email and do some research for an essay I'm writing for college. My laptop is doing some crazy stuff so I have to get it looked at... you know, life is crazy. Is there any way we can maybe pay for temporary use or just access a guest account?" Anna smiled her brightest smile and touched the man's arm to Andrew's dismay, but the desk clerk — with flushed cheeks — agreed to letting them use guest accounts.

"Thank you, doll," Anna said flirtatiously before focusing on one of the computer screens at the terminal the clerk escorted them to.

Andrew was dumb-struck. He'd never seen this side of Anna, manipulating people to get what she wanted.

"What just happened?" he whispered.

"We are in the middle of something huge is what happened," Anna stated. "Don't get stuck on this... let's just figure out what we need and where to find it." She kissed him on the lips reassuringly, much to the chagrin of the observing desk clerk.

"Okay," Andrew exhaled. "Let's do this."

They each got to work on finding what they needed. Andrew focused on the actual equipment and potential places in the area that would have it. Anna researched her symptoms again to make sure she didn't miss anything, and she had to see if any other Morgellons sufferers had experienced lapses in memory. She came up with Alzheimer's for memory issues, but that wasn't what she had.

Once she exhausted symptoms, she started digging into brain science. She researched how the brain functioned and realized that the brain was an organic computer, communicating what it needed to through electrical signals. Of course this was on a microscopic level, but what better way to mess with someone without being obvious? *Too tiny to notice unless you're looking for it,* she thought. *Smart. I wonder if the fibers are even anything close to being organic, or if maybe they were created by someone?*

Andrew was on his own quest to find out what these fibers could possibly be. He had no idea if they were organic material or if there were synthetic attributes, but he figured he should know more. When he first learned about Anna while she was in the psych ward, he'd been the one to analyze the clump of fibers she pulled from her tear duct. He found that the material didn't match any known clothing fabric, which was odd. He even thought to analyze the colored strings against known plants and animal fur. There was no match.

On top of that, Anna had told him about how the ball of fibers reacted when brought near wood, in her case a toothpick. That suggested at least a very basic purpose inherently present in the fibers.

When he researched the disease further online, he came across some theories about nanotechnology, so he made a mental note about that. It wouldn't hurt to be aware of the theories, no matter how conspiratorial or far-fetched they seemed. Their entire situation was far-fetched. Andrew and Anna both knew that they were onto something.

After several hours of scouring the internet for whatever information they could find, the desk clerk interrupted them. *No more untraceable researching,* Anna thought with a sigh.

"Ahem," he cleared his throat. Anna glanced at him. "There are people with library cards who need use of these terminals. Everything is full, so if you'd please finish up?"

"Sure," Anna said, smiling. Her eyes hurt from such intense staring at the screen, but she felt like she had learned a lot... for the time being, anyway.

Andrew just nodded his head as he gathered his notes and closed the browser windows on the screen.

As they left, Anna slipped her hand into his and walked closer to him.

"I'm happy we're in this together," she said. They got into the SUV and headed back to the house to compare notes before they did anything else. It was late and they would probably need to take this up in the morning.

∞

Anna and Andrew both knew what they had to do in order to find out what was really behind these fibers and this so-called disease. So, the next morning, Andrew did something he normally would never do... he called in a favor from a friend based on where the best equipment was located.

"Jake?" Andrew said into his cell phone and paused. Anna listened to one side of the conversation as she sipped her second cup of coffee.

"I hate to do this, but I need a favor," Andrew said with a hint of shame. Anna smiled at his chivalry, but wondered briefly if there was more to it.

"You know I normally wouldn't ask, but this is pretty major," he continued, urgency outweighing his ego. "Anna and I are really close to figuring out what these Morgellons fibers actually are, but we need certain... provisions to be sure."

Andrew had told Anna that Jake was a night watchman at a large research facility in Tacoma, which she didn't think much of until after they'd realized the hospital's equipment wasn't nearly as advanced as the equipment they would need to figure this out. She bit her lip, waiting to see Andrew's reaction about whether his friend would help them or not.

"Okay... I understand," Andrew said. "Of course, that's fine... yes, let's meet now," he finished, grinning broadly and hanging up his phone. He turned to Anna, who was smiling.

"Will he help us?" she asked.

"Well," Andrew began, "he didn't agree to anything yet because he wants to know what's going on." Anna's smile faded. "But if I know Jake Jones, he'll come through for us, especially once he hears some of what's happened so far."

"So we're going now?"

"Yep... we're going now."

∞

As the couple entered the research building, Anna gasped at its vastness self-consciously. This place was riddled with security cameras, and as they walked around, they knew it was for good reason. Jake wore his security badge and served as their guide, still wearing his uniform from his shift the previous night.

"Hey, Phil!" Jake said, smiling at the front desk clerk and showing his badge.

"Hey, Jake! I thought you only came out at night," Phil joked, laughing heartily.

"Yea, so did I," Jake replied with a chuckle. "These are a couple of friends of mine," he said, turning to Anna and Andrew, who smiled and shook hands with Phil. "They asked me to take them on a little tour of where I work, and since this big shot is a doctor, I figured he needed to be a little humbled again," he joked.

"This place certainly does the trick," Andrew said with a good-natured smile.

"Ah, a doctor! Well, good. Now you can see some of what goes on behind the scenes of your profession," Phil said with an earnest smile on his aging, dark-skinned face.

"Perfect," Andrew said, and Jake led the way toward the first department.

"We need to look at a few places on this floor before we can go anywhere else, but talk as you walk," Jake said as people in lab coats passed by them.

"Alright," Andrew said. Anna listened as Andrew spoke with his friend, following them while taking in the equipment and the ceiling-high windows. "We did some more research and found out a few things about Morgellons," Andrew said in a hushed tone. "There's a good chance that these fibers are more than a random disease, and in order to find that out for sure, we need a really strong microscope... way stronger than the lab at the hospital has."

"Really? You guys are that outdated over there?" Jake asked, furrowing his dark eyebrows. Andrew nodded.

"The thing is, every time we try to ask questions or get close to learning more, something weird happens to stop it. Did you know that the FBI told Anna that I was dead?" Andrew asked. Jake's jaw dropped.

"What?!" he whispered harshly. "Dead? I was wondering why I didn't hear from you for so long. When were you gonna tell me this?" he asked.

"I just did," Andrew said simply.

"Well, nobody told *me* anything. You'd think they would look into your past or something—"

"Not the point," Andrew cut him off. "The point is that weird stuff has been happening and I think it's more than we realize. Anna's memory is being affected," he added.

"Her memory? How?" Jake asked. "You know I was in med school with Andrew," he added for Anna's clarification. She gave him a confused look. "I had to drop out because it got too expensive," he said. Anna just nodded, twirling her brown hair in her fingers.

"She forgot her way home from the store about three or four blocks from her house recently," Andrew said. "I don't know if it's going to get worse or not, but once was more than enough for someone who doesn't have Alzheimer's," he added.

Jake gave them both a somber look, his brown eyes softening.

"If we do this, you know I could lose my job," he said plainly. Anna and Andrew nodded. "And that I might get into some real trouble because of some of the research they do here?" They nodded again. "It sounds like you two are into some pretty weird stuff," he added jokingly. Andrew smiled.

"I knew you'd come through," he told Jake.

"Yea, yea... let's just hope we all live to tell the tale," he said as he led them into the elevator. "Now for the real treat," he said with a grin, pressing the button for basement level three.

∞

"Wow," Anna breathed as they entered a huge laboratory with state-of-the-art equipment set up neatly in various glass-enclosed cubicles. There was no one else around. "What is this place?"

"This," Jake announced grandly, walking backwards with outstretched arms, "is where the magic happens!"

"An anatomy lab," Andrew told Anna. He looked around, getting excited as he was reminded of his days in college. "This is where people come to figure out how someone died, or in a lot of cases, to teach medical students or professionals about the human body in a controlled setting," he added. Anna frowned and made a face.

"You mean they bring actual corpses here?" she asked, suddenly a little uneasy.

"Yea," Jake answered her with an excited smile. "Sometimes the FBI takes over this space for a murder case if they can't determine what killed the person."

"Wow," she replied, respect slowly surpassing her uneasiness.

"So is this where some of the equipment is?" Andrew asked. Jake nodded.

"What you want is over here," he said, leading them to the far corner of the lab. He stopped in front of a massive machine with a computer screen and keyboard right next to it. Anna had no idea what she was looking at.

"Oh, wow," Andrew said, running his hand across the top of the machine, which stood almost as tall as he did. "It's a mass spectrometer," he grinned.

"Oh, yes," Jake said matter-of-factly with a huge smile. "This baby will tell you exactly what compounds are in those fibers of yours, and you can go from there."

Anna looked back and forth between both of them, shaking her head in amusement.

"Okay, you guys realize that both of you have massive amounts of geek showing right now, right?" she joked, thankful to be surrounded by friends who knew what they were talking about. She was grateful not to be alone on her journey, and that thought led to that much more gratitude for Andrew.

"Don't knock the geek," Andrew told her playfully, pulling her in for a quick kiss. Jake just smiled.

"But wait," he said with a dramatic pause, "there's more!"

He led them to another machine, this one with a large cylindrical tower and another computer monitor. It looked like there were binoculars attached to the cylinder, but Anna kept her mouth shut and let the geeks do their thing.

"Are you serious?" Andrew asked. "This is perfect!"

"I know," Jake stated with another big smile, enjoying Andrew's enthusiasm.

"This," Andrew said to Anna, "is an electron microscope, which is the most powerful microscope in existence today. Even if the mass spectrometer doesn't recognize the compounds in the fibers, we'll be able to look at them under this and see a lot more than what I was able to before."

Anna beamed. She *knew* they'd be able to figure out what the fibers were now.

∞

After saying goodbye to Jake, the couple returned home to go through their library research one more time and figure out what to do next. Though she seemed calm, Anna was restlessly pacing back and forth in the kitchen, and Andrew worried about what waiting too long would do to her.

"Why don't we go out for lunch today?" Andrew asked in hopes of getting her to calm down.

"Sure, that sounds good," she said, grabbing her coat. "Let's just go do *something*. I'm going stir-crazy over here," she added with a slight smile.

"Alright." They headed out the door and walked to the car where Andrew offered to drive.

"No, no, that's okay," she replied, patting her pockets as she searched for her keys. "Assuming I can find my stupid car keys," she mumbled, checking her coat for the third time. Andrew stood in front of her and lowered her arms gently to her sides.

"Calm down, baby," he whispered in her ear as he reached into her purse and produced the keys. "It's going to be okay," he added for good measure, then kissed her on the forehead lovingly. "Are you sure you don't want me to drive?" he asked again. She relaxed as he touched her.

"I guess that would be best," she said. "I'm pretty wound up right now and I'm not sure why."

"Alright. Hop on in and we'll find somewhere to eat," he said as he smiled at her.

As she opened the passenger side door, she swore she felt someone watching her from across the yard. When she paused to look, there were glowing red eyes staring out from the shadowy entryway of her house. She knew she had to be imagining it, but it didn't *feel* that way.... She looked away and squeezed her eyes shut, then looked back only to watch the eyes slowly disappear backwards into the shadows.

She shook her head and got into the car, sighing as she sat down and buckled her seatbelt. *I must be losing my damn mind*, she thought.

"You okay?" Andrew asked, concerned at her hesitation.

"Yea, I'm fine," she replied. "Let's get something to eat," she added cheerfully. Too cheerful?

As Andrew backed out of the driveway, Anna watched the entry to the house like a hawk. As always, there was nothing there. *Should I finally tell Andrew about these stupid shadows?* she wondered. It wasn't clear to her what she should do, but what was clear was that she felt like she was going crazy, and she still felt alone despite his best efforts and despite knowing how much he cared. What would he do if he thought she was crazy?

"So, where do you want to go?" he asked.

"I'm kinda hungry for seafood," she said. "Maybe that sushi place?" she added. Andrew nodded and drove out of their small town to head toward the larger city of Puyallup nearby.

"Sushi it is," he said with a smile.

They drove in silence for a few minutes as Anna worked up the nerve to confess her delusions.

"Can I tell you something without you thinking I'm certifiable?" she asked. Though she smiled, her tone was somber and he knew something was wrong immediately.

"Of course," he said. "Look at what we're dealing with, right? Conspiracies and a weird, incurable disease... if people think you're crazy, they're bound to think I am." He paused. "Besides... we're in this together. I'm here for you." He placed his hand on her thigh and she covered it with her own.

"Okay," she said, taking a breath. "You know the nightmares I have?"

"Yea, of course," he said.

"I haven't been completely honest with you about them," she said. She took another shaky breath. "I see things when I wake up. No... more like between being asleep and waking up. There are shadowy figures standing all around me, above me... and they're the ones pulling at me."

"Oh, wow," Andrew said, unsure of what else to say. The realization hit him immediately that these might be the 'they' referenced in Jody's suicide note. She'd had nightmares, too, and never told Andrew what they were about.

Anna shifted uncomfortably in her seat.

"Wow, like wow I'm crazy, or *wow*, like you don't know what to say?" she asked. Andrew snapped out of it.

"Wow like I'm not sure what to say," he said. "Do you ever see them when you're awake?" he asked, recalling Jody's strange behavior and what he had thought was exaggerated paranoia at the time.

Anna decided to throw caution to the wind and tell him everything.

"I see them when I'm awake sometimes," she said, aware that his hand had moved away from her thigh as she spoke. *He's driving*, she reassured herself, holding it together with all her might.

"What do they do? What do they look like?" he asked, genuinely curious at that point. He wondered if this whole situation was something they hadn't even considered, something completely different from what they were thinking. His mind flashed to ghosts, spirits, demons, and various other supernatural ideas.

"They're like... people's shadows, but detached from the people they belong to. Some of them have red eyes," she added. "I know how this sounds," she mumbled as an afterthought. Andrew put his hand back on her thigh and smiled at her.

"Anna, don't worry," he said. "I'm still here for you and I still love you just as much as I did before," he said. "But this might be able to clarify a few things that happened with Jody," he added. Anna raised her eyebrows, surprised that he made a connection that no one else had been able to before.

"How do you mean?" she asked, turning toward him in her seat. He was somber.

"I mean... well, she had nightmares, too, and was looking over her shoulder almost constantly when... um... toward the end," he said, uncomfortable at the memories.

"Do you think she saw the shadows, too?" Anna asked, feeling an awkward kinship with Jody.

"I... I think she might have," he said. "It would explain some of the things she said, how she acted, and why she was so scared of what I thought was nothing at the time." Anna squeezed his hand, a tear of relief sliding down her cheek. *He doesn't think I'm crazy... and I'm not alone after all,* she thought. "I think... I think it might explain her suicide note, too," he said softly. Anna just nodded, letting her silent tears fall freely.

"Do you think they're real?" she asked after regaining her composure.

"The shadows?"

"Yea."

"Honestly... at this point, I could believe it if they were."

Chapter Thirteen

"The whole idea is to go in at night so there's less of a chance of someone being there," Jake argued.

"Dude," Andrew countered, "can't you just find out when the lab is mostly empty one day so we can go in and do it in plain sight? B&E 101 says that you look way more suspicious at night, am I right?" He looked to Anna for agreement.

"Don't look at me," she said, raising her hands. "I have never broken into anywhere, so I have no idea!" She busied herself with cooking what she referred to as 'linner' because it was between lunch and dinner time.

"I don't know, man," Jake said, taking a sip of his iced tea. "I'm pretty nervous about this whole thing, and the less people see, the better off we are."

"What about the security cameras?" Andrew asked. "They'll see us no matter what, and we'll stick out a lot more if it's at night and we're the only people going into the building." Jake nodded.

"You know, you might be right," he said after a pause. "So... what if we go back claiming that Anna forgot her cell phone or something in the building somewhere on our tour? Would that work?"

"Do they have a janitor?" Andrew asked.

"Sort of... a cleaning crew comes twice a week..." he paused again as his eyes widened. "... at night. At *night!* The cleaning crew!"

"You're a genius," Andrew said excitedly, his blue eyes lighting up. "What cleaning company is it?" he asked.

"Some industrial cleaning company... they specialize in ordinary cleanup as well as handling caustic chemicals and biohazard stuff. They're called something like... Bio-Industry Services, I think."

"Alright," Andrew said. "When is their next day to go in?"

"They usually show up after closing at about ten on Wednesdays and Saturdays. On my shift."

"Any chance we can... I dunno, hijack their van and equipment on one of those days? And their uniforms?"

"That's so much worse than just committing one crime..." Jake muttered.

"What else can we do? I mean it would definitely be a great way to make sure we have the time we need and go in and out without suspicion. Maybe we can go in on Sunday and say the other team missed a few rooms that we were assigned to handle."

"That still leaves the problem of the uniforms," Jake said, shaking his head. He was liking this less and less. He'd be the one to let them in, so if anything went wrong, it was his job... or worse.

"Here's what their so-called uniforms look like," Anna interjected with a bemused smile, turning her laptop toward them. They all burst out laughing.

"Seriously, all they wear is yellow biochem suits and dust masks? We can get those from the hospital. They have tons of those things in storage and never use them unless there's some kind of quarantine situation, which rarely happens." Andrew was buzzing with excitement.

"Jeez, babe, are you excited to solve our mystery or are you looking forward to sneaking around and getting away with a crime?" Anna joked.

"You're right," Jake said. "We have those at the lab, too. They're exactly the same," he added.

"Alright, a plan is taking shape!" Andrew exclaimed, and Anna shared his excited hope despite herself. She just hoped they could get everything they needed and pull this stunt off without getting caught.

"So... who's responsible for stealing the masks and coveralls?" Jake asked nervously.

"I can get them from the hospital," Andrew replied. "The nurses won't think anything about seeing me because, like you, Jake, they were never informed of my supposed death, I'm sure. I'll be in and out, and I'll probably go at night so not a whole lot of people are there."

Jake breathed a sigh of relief and Andrew laughed.

"For a minute there I thought you'd ask me," Jake said. "The lab keeps tight tabs on those things, so it would definitely be better for you to go grab them," he added.

"No problem," Andrew said. The three of them sat down to eat and changed the subject so they could all relax for a little while before Andrew left that night to go get their supplies.

∞

"Well hi, Dr. Peterson!" a nurse walking past Andrew exclaimed as she stopped to shake his hand. "I haven't seen you in a while! How have you been doing?"

"I've actually been great," Andrew replied with a smile, shaking her hand politely. He had no idea who she was. "I'm on sabbatical," he added, fiddling with the roll of packaging tape in his coat pocket and readjusting the shoulder strap of the messenger bag he had with him.

"I know, I heard!" she exclaimed. *She seems* way *too excited*, he thought. "Let me tell you, rumors have been flying about why you left, but of course that's none of my business," she said with a pouty look, goading him to give her some gossip.

"That's exactly right," he said, "it's not. I'm just here for a minute," he said as he shook her hand again, smiled politely, and left, shaking his head. He wandered the halls for a little while, making sure he wasn't being followed.

As he made his way to the basement where the excess storage room was, he kept a watch in the mirrors and tried to seem as natural as possible. The mirrors may not have been reflecting much, but some of the halls had security cameras, so he knew he had to be as nonchalant as possible.

This particular storage room was where they kept the overflow of supplies that hadn't been used to restock the other supply rooms yet. While the others were only accessible with a code and employee ID, this one was where staff haphazardly threw new shipments of supplies still in their boxes until someone came back to restock the more easily accessible supply rooms.

Once he got to some of the less-accessed areas, he knew there were no cameras. Patients never went down there and most staff didn't, either. He got to the storage room's door and opened it. It wasn't even locked.

As he glanced at all the boxes in the room, he knew he would have to open some of them to see what was inside, especially if there were no labels. *I hope nobody comes down here on the* one *day that something weird is going on*, he thought as he opened one box after another. After checking the contents of each one, he pulled the tape from his pocket and resealed them so no one would be the wiser unless they decided to examine the boxes closely.

Finally, after opening and sealing six boxes, he came across one with the yellow disposable plastic coveralls he was looking for. He hoped they were the kind with hoods as he remembered from the one time he'd had to wear one on shift, and they were. He took out four, just in case, then sealed the box again. He crammed the suits into his messenger bag and searched more boxes for dust masks.

He was sealing box ten when he heard muffled laughter from down the hall. Unwilling to risk getting caught, he slipped out of the storage room and walked a short distance down the hallway to a back exit, where he stepped into the parking garage and stood for a moment to listen with the door cracked.

As the nurses walked by, he heard snippets of their conversation. *Great*, he thought, rolling his eyes. It was the nurse he'd run into starting the gossip chain about him having been spotted in the hospital. *It could be worse*, he thought. *She could be following me to see what I'm really up to.* He found himself briefly grateful for small-minded people. *Looks like Roosevelt's wife was right*, he smirked.

As their voices faded into the distance, he deliberated on whether he should go back in or just buy some dust masks. He could always pay cash, that way no one would be able to tell who bought them... just as a precaution.

Having decided that the safest course of action was a cash purchase, he fished his wallet out of his pocket and checked to see how much he had. Only a twenty, but that would do just fine. *You chickenshit!* The proverbial devil on his shoulder poked at his ego with a tiny red pitchfork. He ignored it and headed across town to a massive pharmacy he'd never been to before... again, just in case.

∞

"Did you get our supplies?" Anna asked excitedly after attacking Andrew with a hug and kisses when he walked into the house. "I was so worried! But you're okay... and you got the yellow suits?" she asked. He chuckled and nodded his head.

"Yes, of course," he told her, embracing her and setting his bag down. "I ended up buying the dust masks because these gossipy nurses came walking by... it wasn't a problem," he finished.

"Oh, gossipy nurses, huh?" Anna asked playfully. "Were they gossiping about you, by chance?"

"Actually, they were," he laughed. "I ran into one of them and told her I was on sabbatical, just stopping by to pick something up. She must have thought that was exciting news."

Anna shook her head. "It's so funny what some people find important these days," she giggled. "Reminds me of that quote about average, simple, and great minds." They shared a laugh and Andrew felt extremely close to her in that moment. That quote had been the first thing he thought of, too. *Roosevelt's wife.*

"Alright... so when do we want to do this?" Anna asked.

"I think I want to call Jake again to figure that out for sure," he said.

"Sounds good," Anna replied. "Tell him he can come over for dinner tomorrow. I'll make something delicious and we can talk before he goes back to work," she added.

"I'll do all that tomorrow sometime," Andrew said with a yawn. "For now, it's late and I'm beat," he added, wrapping his arms around Anna.

"I'm right there with you," Anna said with a smile, returning his embrace. "Let's get some sleep and we can get back to all the craziness tomorrow."

With that, they made their way upstairs to the bedroom.

∞

The next afternoon, Andrew disappeared into the living room for a few minutes as he talked to Jake on the phone and Anna got to work in the kitchen. She decided to make something simple but delicious and filling: a crustless quiche. She mixed the eggs together and let them sit in a bowl in the fridge while she chopped vegetables and fried a package of bacon.

"Alright," Andrew said with a sigh. "So, he ended up lying to Tracy about where he was going and he feels horrible about it, so you can expect to get a little grief from him on the subject," he told her.

"His fiancée? Oh, that sucks... what did he tell her?" Anna asked, hoping it wasn't anything too outlandish.

"He didn't *exactly* lie.... He said he was meeting with us for dinner to discuss wedding plans, more specifically where we want to be on the seating chart... and what you think of the bridesmaid dresses?"

"Oh, no wonder she got mad," Anna said with a laugh. Andrew furrowed his eyebrows. "Her wedding plans are *her* decision," she explained. "No other woman, unless specifically selected by the bride herself, should *ever* give her input on that, especially when that input is unsolicited. He would have been better off sticking with the seating chart thing," she said.

"Why?" Andrew asked, still confused.

"Because she's probably been planning this wedding since she was a little girl," Anna said.

"What?" Andrew was still confused. "She didn't even know who she was going to marry when she was a little girl, how could she possibly plan her wedding from such a young age?" he asked.

Anna sighed. "It's a girl thing," she said. "Lots of little girls dream about their wedding day. Just trust me when I say that the best thing for me to do is either give a compliment or no opinion at all," she finished.

"Alright... if you say so," he said. "Women are weird," he added, and she laughed.

"Tell me something I don't know!" she said, tossing a small chunk of onion at him.

"Hey! Don't waste perfectly good food on my shirt," he joked and sprinted into the kitchen where he embraced her and gave her a kiss.

"Are you weird like that, too?" he asked, seeing a sparkle in her eye.

"I'm a different kind of weird," she said, knowing exactly what he was getting at. "You'll have to find out for yourself to be sure, though," she added with a grin.

"Oh, will I now?" he asked, giving her another kiss and letting her get back to cooking. "Do you want some wine?" he asked her.

"Of course!" she said with a grin, and he got them both glasses.

As he was opening the bottle, the doorbell rang.

"That's Jake," he said and went to open the door.

It wasn't Jake.

Chapter Fourteen

"Anna? Anna!" Casey's familiar voice rang out through the house.

"Casey!" Anna met her friend halfway down the hall. "What are you doing here?" she asked.

"Ugh, you wouldn't believe the week I've had," Casey began. "I just really needed some down time, so I brought the kids to my mom's and decided to drop by to see what you're up to tonight," she added. Anna shot Andrew a significant look. Casey caught it.

"Am I... interrupting something?" she asked Anna.

"Not exactly," Anna said tentatively, trying to figure out what she could say that wouldn't arouse suspicion. "Andrew's friend is coming over to talk about his fiancée's wedding plans and our seating arrangements," she said, going with the same lie that Jake had told. She figured that was the best way for everyone to be on the same page.

"Oh, okay. Nothing too personal or private then, right? I thought for a minute that I was interrupting some kind of proposal or something," she blurted, then covered her mouth with her hand as her eyes widened. "Not that... you know, you probably.... Okay, never mind. I'm digging myself a hole right now, so I'm gonna shut up," she said, but she never blushed. Anna laughed.

"You are by far the most unfiltered person I know," she said, still giggling. She led her friend to the kitchen where she got a third glass of wine out and offered it to Casey, who nodded vigorous approval.

"What are you cooking?" Casey asked, looking at all of the ingredients on the counter. Anna finished cutting up some red bell peppers, crumbled the now-crunchy bacon, and took the bowl of eggs out of the fridge.

"You wanna take a guess?" Anna asked with a wink.

"Hm... well, it's either omelets or quiche," she said. "Or one of your weirdly delicious spin-offs of either one," she added with a smile and a wink.

"Crustless quiche," Anna announced softly, "and I got the recipe online," she added. Casey laughed and took a few sips of her wine.

"Amazing," she said. "I've had your crustless quiche before and it was delicious," she added. "Can I have more wine?" she asked. Anna shook her head in amusement, hoping that Casey didn't plan on driving.

"You can have as much as you want, as long as you promise to crash on our couch," she stated.

"Not to worry," Casey said. "The kids are there overnight, so I'm a free woman!" She clinked glasses gently with Anna and sat down on a stool next to the island. She watched as Anna dumped all of the ingredients into a glass baking dish and mixed it around, then sprinkled shredded cheese on top before putting it in the oven.

"I love how simple your food is," Casey said. "Like... you take what's familiar to the palate and turn it into something delicious without overcomplicating it," she said. Anna was always glad when Casey appreciated her cooking, since Casey was a much more sophisticated eater than she had ever been.

"Well, thank you," Anna said with a smile. She sat down on the other stool at the island and they sipped their wine together.

"I speak the truth," Casey stated, and Anna could see the wine slowly beginning to take effect. It wasn't that Casey was slurring her words or anything; she just got more relaxed and let go of some of her chaos. Anna liked her calmness when she had a few drinks. It was like the alcohol melted away her stress and she was allowed to unwind for a while.

"What's been going on with you, anyway?" Anna asked. "I haven't seen you since... well, never mind since," she finished, shooting Andrew a look that said she remembered but forgave him.

"I've been a little freaked out, actually," Casey said. "Since that Tom or whoever he was incident, I don't really think I should trust any men who randomly approach me. I think I need to work through what happened first," she finished.

"I agree. That's probably for the best."

"What about you? Anything exciting going on with you and lover boy?" she asked mischievously.

Anna turned a little pink. "No, not really," she said modestly. "We're just... us. And it's nice."

"Just nice, huh? Get rid of him," Casey winked jokingly.

"My ear is itching, do I hear girly talk about me in here?" Andrew came into the kitchen with his empty wine glass. He grabbed the bottle and gently swirled what was left of it in circles. "Wow, you ladies hit this kinda hard, didn't you?" he asked jokingly.

"Well, considering that one bottle usually doesn't contain more than three or four full glasses, I think we're okay," Casey said and smacked him on the arm jokingly. "I know you have a stash somewhere, Anna," Casey added with a laugh. "I am going to get completely and utterly fucked up tonight. I deserve it. My kids are nuts, life is nuts, and I think I just need to enter oblivion," she added. "Not to mention sleeping in.... oh my God, sleeping in and actually *really* sleeping!"

Anna knew that her friend wouldn't talk about what was bugging her until she was well on her way to sloshed, so she wasn't going to stop her. If anything, she would encourage it a little so she could give her some solid advice over breakfast the next morning.

"Bring on the stash!" Anna said boisterously, raising her glass and glancing at Andrew to bring another bottle in.

Just then, the doorbell rang.

"Okay, now *that's* Jake," Anna said as she got up to answer the door. Casey stayed in her seat, waiting for a proper introduction.

"I'm so mad at you two," Jake said half-jokingly to Anna as she opened the door and put her finger to her lips.

"Don't go into anything crazy quite yet," she whispered as she gave him a hug to greet him. "My friend Casey dropped by unexpectedly," she added. Jake composed himself, clearly weirded out by the whole situation.

"What smells so good?" he asked Anna a little loudly. She gave him a look.

"Seriously? Has no one taught you how to pretend things are fine?" she asked in a hushed tone.

"I suck at lying," he said plainly. "Why do you think I'd rather Tracy be pissed about the bridesmaid thing than me lying? It totally took the attention off of me."

Anna couldn't help but let out a laugh. *Brilliant!* she thought. She put a hand on his shoulder and led him to the kitchen, where the quiche was beginning to fill the house with its delicious aroma and Casey sat finishing her glass of wine. She smiled at Jake as Anna introduced them.

"Casey, Jake... Jake, Casey," Anna said just as Andrew came back from the garage with four bottles of wine.

"Whoa, dude," Jake said with his hands up, "I do *not* need that much liquid courage to talk about seating arrangements," he joked.

"Ah, but apparently Casey and Anna do," Andrew stated with a wink at Anna, who smiled as she opened a new bottle and filled Casey's glass as well as her own. It wouldn't be the worst idea for her to get drunk with her friend while Andrew and Jake discussed the real matter at hand. Then Anna could get Casey talking about some of her man issues to distract her while the guys talked about covertly using the equipment at the lab.

Andrew squeezed Casey's shoulder comfortingly and leaned down to tell her softly, "I hope things are okay with you," knowing that whatever was driving her to drink might have to do with what had happened with James.

"Oh, I'm fine," Casey replied with a dismissive little wave. "Honestly, I just don't want to think about my life at all anymore today. Please tell me you guys have something exciting going on," she added, desperate for a distraction.

Anna put a hand gently on her friend's arm before getting up to lead Andrew to the living room.

"Can we please tell her?" she asked him quietly. "I know it's like a top secret thing and I didn't really want to get her involved, but I hate lying to her. I hate that I've been so detached from her and that she doesn't know the full extent of everything that's going on," she added.

Andrew sighed. He knew she needed to confide in her friend, but a part of him – the part that was supposed to be following the rules of the BQS and playing his role in whatever they were really doing – knew that this whole thing was destined to fall apart... or worse. The more people knew, the less secure any information was. And what if James had gotten to Casey and turned her? If that happened to be the case, she would definitely turn on him, even if he was her best friend's boyfriend.

"Okay," he said finally. If Casey *had* been turned, it was a good opportunity for him to come clean to Anna about everything... the *real* everything.

Anna gave him a big hug and walked back to the kitchen quickly, where she was a little surprised to see Casey and Jake talking like they were old friends. *Uh oh*, Anna thought. She didn't know Tracy, but she knew Casey... and how charming she could be. She hoped that Jake wasn't that kind of man, although she also hoped that Casey would finally find someone good for her. Their body language spoke volumes, though.

"Good news!" Anna announced as she settled back into her chair and took her turn downing the rest of her glass of wine. She poured herself a new one and topped off all the others. Jake was beginning to warm up to the idea of relaxing, so he accepted a glass, too.

"Okay...?" Casey asked, her curiosity piqued.

"I can tell you what's really going on," Anna said just as Andrew walked in and nodded at Jake, whose expression had briefly changed to one of alarm.

Casey froze. "I *knew* there was something going on with you!" she exclaimed. "What is it? Did he propose? Are you moving? What is it?" She could barely contain her excitement.

Anna laughed. "No, no! Nothing like that," she stated with a smile, but her smile faded. "It's actually... more bad and weird news than good news," she confessed.

"Now I'm really intrigued, but also a little scared. What is it?" Casey asked. Jake fidgeted nervously.

"It's... kind of a long story, but I think we can get through it, right guys?" Anna looked to Andrew and Jake for approval, and while Andrew gave it, Jake was still a wreck.

"You guys know my job is on the line for this crap, right?" he blurted out suddenly. "And if Tracy ever found out, she would *kill* me," he added. "Not figuratively, but *literally* kill me and burn my body and then bury the bones in random places all over the country," he emphasized.

Anna furrowed her brows, as did Casey.

"Jesus, your fiancée sounds *scary*," Anna stated with a worried look on her face. "You're going to marry a woman you're afraid of?" she asked. She looked at Andrew, wondering if he felt the same way about her. Seeming to read her mind, he smiled reassuringly and moved in to give her a gentle kiss on her forehead.

"Of course I am! You women are *all* crazy," Jake stated. He was trying to pass it off as a joke, but Anna could tell he truly felt that way. She raised her eyebrows.

"I think you've been meeting the wrong kind of women," she said simply. After a short pause, she continued. "Back to the matter at hand, although your psychological issues clearly need some work," she joked. Smile fading, she turned to Casey. "We have a problem," she said. "My disease is not only incurable, but it has all sorts of weird side-effects and the stuff that comes out of my sores is not identifiable by the hospital's mediocre equipment," she said. Casey's eyes widened.

"What is it, then?" she asked. Andrew jumped in.

"We think it's some kind of top secret technology or something biological that hasn't been dealt with before, at least not publicly or that we can find out anything about online," he said. "Honestly, we have no idea what it is. That's what we're trying to figure out," he added.

"Get this," Anna interjected. "Andrew was a part of a group where they would pay him thousands of dollars for a single sample of Morgellons fibers. These people call themselves the Bureau of Quantum Sciences, and no one is allowed to see anyone else's face. And... Tom was involved, but his name is really James," she added. Casey's jaw dropped.

"You guys are seriously in the middle of an *actual* conspiracy, aren't you?" she asked. "Man! This is exactly what I was talking about! This! *This* is the kind of excitement I need! And what the hell with the Tom-James thing? Ugh, the crazies always pick me, don't they? Anyway, beside the point. Tell me more," she finished excitedly as she took another sip of her wine. Casey's need for adventure not involving her kids seemed to be taking over her logic. Or it could've been the wine.

"Jake here," Anna said, looking at Jake, "has access to a state of the art lab with all the latest equipment including—"

"An electron microscope and a mass spectrometer machine," Jake interjected, knowing Anna might not remember the names of the machines. He chugged his glass of wine, then refilled it and drank half of that glass. "I'm so dead," he mumbled, finishing off the glass. He refilled again.

"We're gonna sneak in and use the equipment by posing as the cleaning crew," Anna finished, her eyes alive with the adrenaline pumping through her veins.

Casey was astounded. "You. *You*... are gonna commit a *crime?*" she asked Anna, amazed.

"I don't see it as a crime, *per se*...." Anna trailed off, feigning innocence.

"You're going into a facility you're not allowed to be in posing as the cleaning crew to use their expensive equipment... and that's not a crime?" Casey asked, a smile playing on her lips. Anna didn't know what to say.

"Can I come with you?" Casey asked after a pause. They all exchanged glances and nodded their agreement after a moment of deliberation. Anna felt relieved, not only to have told her friend but also that she was on board, although a big part of her also wondered if she had made the right choice.

∞

As the morning wore on, Anna became more and more anxious. They were supposed to go into the lab tonight, and she didn't know whether she wanted to puke or dance. Her emotions were all over the place and she couldn't help but entertain ideas of getting caught versus absolute success in identifying what the fibers were made of. Her brain didn't know which direction to lean in, which caused chaos throughout the rest of her body... mostly her stomach and gag reflex.

"Are you ready for tonight?" Casey asked from across the kitchen island where she sat with a cup of coffee. She didn't even seem fazed at the thought, much less by the amount of wine she'd consumed the night before. *How does she* do *that?* Anna wondered.

"Honestly? No," Anna stated, her nausea and nervousness apparent all over her face. "I'm nervous, I'm nauseated, I'm freaking out, and all I wanted was to figure out what's really wrong with me," she confided. "I feel like I want to puke," she finished.

Casey had a sympathetic look on her face as she got up and approached her friend to give her a comforting hug.

"Honey... this idea came about because you had no choice. I know there are a lot of potential outcomes, but let's focus on the best one for now, okay?" she said. "I'm nervous, too," she added. "Just a bit more excited than nervous because my kids are taken care of and I have a little freedom for a few days because my mom volunteered to keep them longer. And what better way to use that freedom than by helping my best friend figure out the truth? The truth is a noble cause," she finished.

"You're right," Anna replied, smiling. Casey was an emotional train wreck sometimes, but she really knew how to turn a crime into a noble cause, didn't she? "I need to stop thinking in what ifs and start focusing on the plan, that way things go as they're supposed to and we don't mess up everything we've worked for."

"Absolutely!" Casey said, going back to her coffee. "We literally planned this whole thing out and went over it about thirty times last night, so we should be able to pull it off without any problems, right?" Anna wasn't sure whether Casey was trying to convince herself or Anna, but she would take it.

"Any word from Jake or Andrew this morning?" Anna asked.

"No... was Andrew still sleeping when you came down?" Casey asked.

"Of course," Anna said with a smile.

"Silly boys, can't even handle a few glasses of wine, right?" Casey laughed. Anna grinned as they heard Andrew making his way down the stairs and both women burst into a fit of giggles.

"Ah, I see the lushes are still feeling pretty good," Andrew commented as he rubbed his forehead with his fingers. "Coffee?" he asked, squinting at Anna.

Anna poured him a cup of black coffee and handed it to him. "Lushes, huh?" she asked, giggling again.

"I think I'm still a little drunk," Casey remarked, laughing along with Anna.

"Me, *too!*" Anna said, and they both burst into giggles again.

"You two are alone on that front," Andrew stated with a wince. "Anybody know what happened to Jake last night?" he asked.

"No," Anna said, her expression becoming serious. "Did he *drive* like that?" she asked, hoping the answer was no.

"Nope.... I'm here!" The three of them looked toward the stairs in time to hear a stomp, a stumble, a crashing sound, and Jake unevenly walking down the stairs.

"Hey, are you okay, man?" Andrew asked, concerned. "Where the hell did you sleep, anyway?" he added, truly curious.

"Your shower curtain is kinda... not up anymore," Jake said, holding onto the railing for dear life. "Did you know that bathtubs make terrible beds?" he added, limping and leaning against the wall as he made his way to the kitchen.

"Why didn't you take one of the couches?" Anna asked.

"Casey had one couch and I just didn't feel right about it...." Jake answered absent-mindedly. "My fiancée is gonna kill me anyway, so maybe I should have," he added with a laugh.

Clearly, no one was thinking yet.

Casey snorted. "That was the worst line I've ever heard," she said playfully, giving Jake a hard time. He looked at her sheepishly before accepting a cup of coffee from Anna.

"Not a line," he stated between sips. "I'm just saying whatever comes into my head at this point," he added. They all laughed.

Anna suddenly jumped into action, her nervous energy getting the best of her.

"Best hangover cure," she started, "is a phenomenal breakfast and a good Bloody Mary. You guys just sit down and I'll get to work," she said. Casey looked at her with sparkling eyes.

"You're *so* right!" she said, jumping up to help Anna. "I should help," she added. "Why don't you two go enjoy your coffee in the living room with some TV and we'll take care of the hangover cure?" she winked at Jake.

"Fine," Andrew said, neither of them having noticed her winking. Anna had, though.

"What are you doing?" she whispered to Casey. "He's getting *married!*"

"He didn't even *see* that!" Casey argued. "Besides, he needs to realize that not all women are controlling, nag all the time, and expect them to hand over all of their hard-earned money," she added. "You heard how he was talking last night. Alcohol reveals the truth," she said, a mischievous smile playing across her lips. Anna couldn't help but smile back.

"Alright, you've got the whole bitchy thing right, but still! It's just *wrong*," she said. "Just be careful, Casey," she added somberly.

"I'm not even doing anything!" Casey said, mocking shock. "Let's get this breakfast cooked and we'll blow them both away with our culinary prowess," she added with a wink, and they got to work in the kitchen.

"What do you think they're giggling about in there?" Jake asked Andrew after their first cup of coffee. He hoped he didn't make an idiot of himself the night before.

"Who knows?" Andrew asked, unwilling to be a part of the drama... or cause problems, even inadvertently. He knew *exactly* what they were giggling about. "I think Casey likes you and I also think they're offended that you would think all women are crazy. They want to prove you wrong," he added.

"Oh God... did I say all that last night?" Jake asked. Andrew nodded. "No wonder the whole thing felt so weird. I love Tracy... I would never do anything to compromise my relationship with her," he added. "Although I wish she could be more understanding about stuff like tonight.... Oh, no... tonight!" he said, his eyes suddenly getting wide. "We went over that damn plan so many times last night and I don't even remember what the plan *is*," he muttered, rubbing his forehead. "How could I ever have agreed to this?" he asked.

"Dude, calm down," Andrew said. "Remember that it's because no one in any kind of official capacity has given us answers about Anna's disease, and remember, too, that this might lead to something much bigger than the answer to Morgellons."

"Yea...."

"We're doing what's right," Andrew said. "It's not just for Anna, either. What if we find something truly mind-blowing and mysterious when we investigate these fibers? What if it leads to a cure? That would affect tens of thousands of people."

"I guess. I'm just... really uncomfortable about the whole thing should it go wrong. My job, my whole life... I know Tracy would be pissed if she knew what we were up to." Jake sighed.

"End goal," Andrew said. "Keep the end goal in mind and think good thoughts. Let's just enjoy breakfast and a Bloody Mary and get our heads straight first, okay?"

"You're right. I'm just freaking out because this isn't even my cause. It's *your* cause. You're the catalyst for this whole thing," Jake said. "If I lose my job or lose Tracy, then what?"

"You won't lose either," Andrew reassured. "Now knock it off and watch TV," he added with a sympathetic smile.

Chapter Fifteen

They pulled into the parking garage under the building and parked. Everyone had agreed that changing into their stolen coveralls and dust masks before they left was the best option, even though it made them look like asylum escapees during their drive. Luckily it was dark, so they all wordlessly prayed that no one noticed.

The ride to the lab was silent. Jake was at work in the building already, doing whatever it was that he normally did, at least they all hoped so. No one was certain that he would be able to pull off acting natural with how freaked out he'd been for most of the day, but they all had to have faith in one another.

Anna and Casey looked at each other and nodded as Andrew cocked his head to motion for them to get out of the car and head inside. Anna didn't know why they were all so quiet, but it felt like the right thing to do at the time.

The trio made their way to the service entrance and silently prayed for a miracle. Luckily for them, there was only one security guard and he smiled at them like he recognized them.

"Hey, guys! Extra cleaning duty?" he asked, his white teeth gleaming in contrast to his dark olive skin.

"You could say that," Andrew replied with a smile. "It's a huge inconvenience for everybody, but hopefully worth it," he added jokingly.

"Well, I don't know what these lab rats do all the time to create such a mess, but by all means, do your thing!" The security guard seemed visibly disgusted by whatever mental image he got from his own statement, so they all assumed he'd seen them examining a dead body... or worse.

"Do things get pretty crazy around here?" Anna asked curiously.

"Let's just say I'm glad I never became a scientist... or a doctor," he said with a chuckle. They joined in, trying to calm their nerves as they continued on their mission.

"Here we are," the guard said. "You guys do your thing... and have fun! ... Or not, right?" he laughed again. They chuckled but looked at each other with mild dread.

"What the hell are we getting ourselves into?" Casey softly asked Andrew, who just shrugged.

"I have no idea. But whatever it is, we're gonna have to get this place as clean as we can without damaging anything if we want to pull off this little information heist," he added.

Anna and Casey looked at each other skeptically but followed Andrew.

As they walked through the deserted halls they ran into Jake, who was surprisingly calm.

"Well, hello there!" Jake said with a smile. "I hope you're here to handle the mess in the main lab," he added with a wink.

"Of course we are," Andrew said, slightly surprised by Jake's attitude.

Jake leaned in to whisper to Andrew. "I told Tracy everything, she gets it, and there's an actual mess for you guys to clean up, which makes the story rock solid."

"Oh?"

"Human remains... well, what's left of them on the table, anyway. They already took what they needed and catalogued everything, so the goop is all yours."

"Great," Andrew said with a sigh. "Looks like we've got our work cut out for us."

Jake kept walking as he made his rounds and the three of them made their way to the main lab, which also housed the equipment they needed.

As they entered the room, the smell of death infiltrated their noses. It was fairly faint, but still disgusting... and unmistakable.

"We really have to clean all this?" Casey asked as they approached a stainless steel table with chunks of human tissue all over it, some of it burned.

"Burn victim?" Anna asked, trying to adjust to the smell without gagging.

"Looks like," Andrew said, wrinkling his nose. "Can I have a couple of the fiber samples?" he asked, holding a rubber gloved hand out to Anna.

"Sure," she said as she reached into a pocket under her coveralls and pulled out several plastic zippered bags with Morgellons fibers in them. "I hope you plan on helping us with this shit," she added, only half-joking. "How are we supposed to clean up human... goo?" she asked. She had no idea what to do with this mess.

"Yea, Andrew," Casey chimed in. "You're a doctor, how do we clean this stuff up? I've never even *seen* a dead person before... whole or otherwise," she added, making a face. Casey wasn't sure if she should be disgusted, feel pity, or pray. It was a strange ambivalence.

"Gather the tissue that's left and put it in the biohazard disposal unit," he pointed at a weird-looking garbage can across the room, "and then wipe everything down with bleach at least three times." He smiled at the women, knowing he was exempt from waste removal because he was the only one who would be able to identify any results from the sophisticated equipment.

"Damn smart people," Casey said, but then chuckled. "Did you think we'd be cleaning up after a human body when we decided to do this?" she asked Anna, who let out a slight laugh.

"At least it looks like we're serving some kind of legitimate purpose while we do our digging for the truth, right?" Anna nodded at her friend and they got to work as Andrew took the samples and ran each one through the mass spectrometer machine individually.

Andrew watched as he placed each sample into the machine and none of them yielded any conclusive results.

"The mass spectrometer isn't giving me much," he said, wondering how that was even possible. Were there too many compounds to identify? The mass spec machine should have been able to separate them, but it didn't. Why? "The only thing it's telling me is that there are multiple compounds. One seems to be quartz crystal...." he trailed off.

"Try the microscope," Anna said as she wiped down the stainless steel surface one more time with her now-pink rag soaked in bleach solution and blood. She was happy to be wearing gloves, to say the least.

Andrew just nodded and took one of the samples to the electron microscope. He placed the specimen into the device and looked through the microscope lenses, prepared for anything.

What he saw shocked him to some degree as he hadn't expected it. The fibers themselves were moving. Toward him. Like they were drawn to him. But... what was that?

He increased the magnification and realized something else. There *were* tiny crystals all over the fiber, like they were woven into the fibers themselves... embedded. They were small enough to be missed by the naked eye, which made them difficult to detect. What were crystals used for besides cheap jewelry and energy healing practices?

He swiveled in his chair to the computer behind him and typed in 'tiny crystals for medicine' and yielded results on hydroxyapatite crystal disease. He decided to narrow his search for what he suspected – as conspiratorial as it seemed – and typed in 'crystals and technology.' His results yielded all manner of information about data storage on crystal quartz. His mind ran in all kinds of different directions with that information, but he knew he would need some sort of proof of data storage if he was going to do anything about Morgellons and what was causing Anna's disease... and everything that went with it.

"I think we're done here," Casey said as they surveyed the clean area. She looked at Anna mischievously. "Let's go check out the other equipment," she said, and they made their way across the massive room to the other side.

Neither one of them had any idea about what they were looking at, but they were still impressed... and a little intimidated.

"So this is where the geniuses work, huh?" Anna remarked. "I wonder how much all this stuff is worth?" she wondered aloud.

"All the equipment in the lab is worth about three point four million dollars," a male voice interrupted their conversation. Panic flashed in both of their eyes, but the women quickly recovered. "What are you doing here?" he asked.

"Dr. Schwartz!" Anna said with surprise. "I didn't know you worked at this lab," she added, hoping that he wouldn't be too suspicious of her being there. *Who am I kidding? Of course he'll be suspicious!*

"Anna!" Dr. Schwartz said, just as surprised as Anna was. "What are you doing here?" he asked. "I thought you just worked from home?"

"I usually do, but... you know, bills. I needed a temporary position to tide me over," she added with a nervous smile.

"Am I not paying you enough for Sophia's lessons?" he asked, genuinely concerned. Anna racked her brain for a believable answer.

"No, it's not that," she said with a bright smile. "My friend is getting married and I'm saving to get a nice dress," she lied. He smiled and nodded.

"Ah, well good for your friend!" he said. "Pardon me if I don't shake your hand," he added. "I know what goes on here all too well!" They laughed together, but it was short-lived as Dr. Schwartz noticed Andrew using the equipment. *We're screwed,* Anna thought, giving Casey an alarmed look as they watched the doctor walk over to where Andrew was.

"Excuse me!" Dr. Schwartz said loudly, shocking Andrew back to reality. Andrew stood up calmly, wearing a smile behind his dust mask.

"Well, hello!" he said jovially, reaching out to shake the doctor's hand.

"What are you doing with my equipment?" Dr. Schwartz asked.

"I'm sorry," Andrew began, searching his brain for a reason. "My supervisor said I could borrow some equipment here to check on something," he stated. "I take it this means Dr. Adams didn't call you?" He hoped and prayed that his memory of the building's department listings served him well.

"No, of course that bastard didn't call me," Dr. Schwartz said irritatedly. "What are you working on anyway? What is it that we're looking at?" Andrew gulped and hoped that he wouldn't show too much interest.

Dr. Schwartz knew exactly what he was looking at. *Are these Anna's Morgellons fibers he's analyzing?* he wondered. *And who authorized them the use of the lab?* He had specifically found Anna to teach Sophia about art partially because he knew she had the disease. The whole point had been to stay legitimately connected to her, not rouse her suspicions about Morgellons... or his involvement with the disease. He listened as Andrew carefully maneuvered his way out of giving a real answer.

"You know, we aren't exactly sure," Andrew told him, which was partially true. "Someone gave us these samples to analyze to see if we could identify them, but so far we haven't had much luck." Also semi-true.

"Interesting," Dr. Schwartz replied. Dr. Schwartz was torn. On the one hand, he knew he should call security, just to be sure. On the other hand, he wondered if they were in a similar situation as he was, forced into an impossible situation.

"Alright then," Dr. Schwartz said finally, and Andrew breathed a subtle sigh of relief. "Carry on. I certainly hope you figure it out," he added as he made his way toward one of the exits.

"What do you think they're talking about over there?" Casey asked, watching from across the lab with Anna. When Anna didn't reply, she swiveled around to look for her friend and found herself alone.

"Anna?" she called. "Where'd you go?" she asked. Casey heard a heavy door close and followed the sound to check it out. Nervous, she decided to get Andrew before she went any further and began to worry about Anna.

"Andrew?" Casey said softly as she approached him. He was looking into the microscope and had an expression of awe and disbelief on his face.

"Yea," he said, not looking up.

"I don't know where Anna went," Casey said. "One second she was right there and the next she was gone," she added.

"Shit," Andrew said, fearing the worst. "We have to find her. I think I have enough information from the fibers for now. I printed a few pictures from the microscope and emailed a bunch of them to myself." He gathered the fiber samples and shoved them into his bag along with the printed images. He then deleted all of his activity, powered everything down, and joined Casey in trying to find Anna.

"Where could she have gone?" Casey asked as they made their way toward the door she'd heard close.

"I don't know," Andrew replied. "But I'm wondering if maybe she's having another memory lapse. They're been getting worse every time, and closer together... like something's messing with her mind that has to do with the disease."

"Yea, you'd mentioned that," she said, growing more worried. Andrew opened the heavy door and Casey followed him through it. They walked down the dimly lit hallway cautiously, still feeling out of place even though the guards knew they were there and thought they had a legitimate reason to be. Andrew's phone went off. He took it out of his pocket and checked the text message, which was from Jake: 'Found Anna. She doesn't know who I am. What's going on?'

"Uh oh," Andrew mumbled and quickened his pace. Casey kept up. 'Where are you?' he texted Jake back. His phone went off a few seconds later. 'Room 312, down the hall from you,' was Jake's reply.

162

"What's happening?" Casey asked as she followed Andrew down the hall quickly.

"Jake found Anna but she doesn't know who he is," he told her. "I can only hope that she remembers us so we can get her out of here," he added. As they made their way down the hall, he glanced at the room numbers on each door and they finally got to room 312.

"Here it is," he said and tried the doorknob. Locked. He knocked gently on the door and heard shuffling inside.

"Thank God you're here," Jake said, gesturing behind him toward Anna, who was sitting at the desk of a Dr. Wyatt. Andrew had expected her to be a mess, but she seemed calm enough.

"Anna?" he asked as he approached her. "Are you okay?"

"Andrew!" she said happily. "I don't know what happened, but I ran into this crazy guy and he thinks he knows me... and that I'm not supposed to be in this building. At least that's what he told me. I thought you were working?" she asked Andrew, who wondered why her memories were so jumbled. He decided that the best thing was to play along so that he could convince her to leave with him.

"Well, I was and now I'm done," he told her with a smile. "Are you ready to go home?" he asked her.

"Of course," she said with a smile. She looked at Casey and said, "Is this your new assistant?"

"Yep, she's going to be coming back with us," he said before Casey could interject. Casey shook her head in sad disbelief and followed the couple back down to the service entrance. She couldn't believe Anna would remember Andrew but not her. Whatever this disease was doing to her was unlike anything she'd ever seen or heard of. As they approached the service entrance, the guard didn't even bother getting up from his seat as they left; he just waved them through.

The three of them got into the car and Andrew breathed a huge sigh of relief as they turned onto the main road. They'd done it. Now he just needed Anna to snap out of it so that he could tell her what he'd found out about the fiber samples.

"What happened?" Anna said suddenly as they got on the freeway back to Deeplake. "How did we get back into the car? Did you find out what was going on with the fibers?"

"Oh, you're back," Andrew said with a relieved smile.

"Good!" Casey chimed in from the back seat. "Now I can stop pretending to be your new assistant," she chuckled.

"Assistant?" Anna asked. "What are you doing here, Casey?"

"What? You're kidding, right?" Casey asked.

"I am so confused," Anna said. "What's going on?" she asked.

"Stay calm," Andrew told her. "You forgot where we were and didn't remember Jake at all," he began.

"Who's Jake?"

Andrew furrowed his brows.

"Why don't you tell me what you *do* know and I can piece the rest together for you after that?" he suggested. Anna sighed, but nodded.

"I know we were at that lab so you could examine the fibers with their equipment. I remember cleaning up, and then nothing. I don't know who Jake is and I thought it was just you and me at the lab, which is why it seems weird to me that Casey is here," she finished.

"Okay," Andrew began. "Jake is my best friend. He works at the lab as a night watchman and got us in under the pretense of cleaning up hazardous materials. Casey came with us and she helped you clean up the lab while I looked at the fibers. You must still be having some kind of memory lapse."

"Seems that way," she said, shaking her head and breathing deeply. She needed to focus on something else. "Did you find anything out about the fibers?"

"Yes, actually," he began. "They're attracted to organic materials as far as I can tell, and they'll actually move on their own. But something even stranger is that they aren't just fibers. There are tiny little crystals woven into them, which I needed to confirm before bringing it up to you."

"What does that mean?" Casey asked.

"This is gonna sound like I'm a conspiracy theory nut, but it's possible to use crystals as a means for data storage," he said. "Can you imagine what that might mean if all Morgellons fibers have the capability to collect and store data?"

"Is there a way to see what data might be on those crystals?" Anna asked.

"There's a device similar to a tablet that can read the data on crystals, but they have to be the right shape and size... and it's an extremely new and expensive technology. I think we might be able to improvise on that, though," Andrew said.

"If all Morgellons fibers can store information, who's that information going to after it's stored?" Casey asked.

"That's something I don't know," Andrew said. "What I do know is that I was being paid quite a bit for every fiber sample I turned over to the Bureau of Quantum Sciences. I never saw anyone's face and everything was completely anonymous. What they did with it after that is beyond me."

"When was the last time you went and turned over a fiber sample?" Anna asked.

"It's been a while. When they were holding me hostage they asked me to start again, but I haven't gone back. I could, though. Maybe we should talk to James."

"Tom? Fuck. That sucks," Casey said. "I really was hoping never to have to deal with that douche-bag again." She sighed.

"Sorry, Casey," he said. "But he might be our best lead... we need to find a way to access the information that might be on those crystals."

"Is that kind of technology even in existence?" Anna asked.

"I don't know," he replied. "I just read about it recently and I don't think it's widely available, but we may be able to modify a microscope to see what we can see."

"Do you even know what you're looking for?" Casey asked.

"No," Andrew admitted. "But I *do* know that trying is better than not trying."

"That's definitely true," Anna said. "Let's see what we can see," she said with a smile. "In the meantime, though, I think we should take the night off. I'm beat!"

"I hear you there. Me, too," Andrew said as he squeezed Anna's hand.

∞

Anna woke in the middle of the night with her head throbbing. Gently touching her forehead with her hand, she sat up and looked around the dim room. Confused, she wondered what had happened. *Where am I?*

As she racked her brain to remember, to catch a thought – any thought – of what had happened before she went to sleep, she noticed that there were shadows moving all around her. There had to be some kind of moving light for them to be doing that, but she couldn't tell where it was coming from. God, her head was pounding....

She slipped out of bed and wandered around the room, looking around but not recognizing a thing. Was this her bedroom? Or had something happened and was she somewhere else?

Finding the light switch, she flipped it on and was astonished to see that the shadows were still there, moving all over the room.

Before her eyes, they transformed from unrecognizable gyrating blobs to tall silhouettes that almost resembled human shadows. One of them had red glowing eyes and looked like it wore a fedora, and she found the shadows to be very familiar. She was slightly surprised that she didn't feel scared; logically, she knew she should, but she didn't. She just watched in fascination as they approached her.

"Who are you?" she asked, standing still.

"You're almost ready," the one with the glowing eyes said. Though the figure had no facial features except for the eyes, she sensed that it was the one speaking. And it wasn't even really speaking out loud... it was more like she heard the voice in her head. Mildly disturbing... but she felt calm.

"Ready for what?" she asked, still unsure of what was going on but curious to learn more.

"You're one of the chosen ones, Anna," it said. "Soon, you'll understand so much more than what you do now."

"Will it hurt?" Anna asked.

"No," it said. As it communicated with her, it moved closer toward her. It was almost touching her, but she intrinsically knew that it couldn't, that it wasn't of this world. "It won't hurt, Anna. You'll simply become more powerful than most humans," it added.

"What do you mean?" she asked. She flinched as she saw movement coming from the bed she'd just gotten up from and a man sat up and squinted at her sleepily. She felt a chill on her skin as the shadow with the glowing eyes seemed to touch her, but it felt more like it passed *through* her.

"Who are you talking to, Anna?" the man in the bed asked her. Her eyes widened.

"Who are you?" she asked him. "And why are you in my bed? Is that even my bed?"

He gave her a concerned look as he sat up and put his bare feet on the floor to stand. Anna backed away, feeling more scared of this person than she had been of the shadow. The shadow had... *felt* familiar. Like she was somehow connected to it.

"Anna," he said sympathetically, reaching his hand out to her. "I'm Andrew. Don't you remember?" he asked. Anna shook her head, but calmed down a little as she realized that he seemed to care about her. "I'm your boyfriend, Anna. You've been sick," he told her. "Your illness is confusing your memories." He spoke gently and she approached him cautiously, taking his outstretched hand. Allowing him to pull her close, she sighed and caught his scent, a gentle mingling of yesterday's Aqua di Gio, sweat, and her own perfume mixed in.

Synapses fired as her mind made the connection in milliseconds, and she began to sob uncontrollably.

"What is happening to me?" she asked between gasps of air as Andrew hugged her tightly. "Did you see the shadow?" she asked, setting off alarms in Andrew's head.

"*Shh*," he said soothingly. "It's going to be okay, Anna. We're gonna figure this out and it will all be okay." She clutched him tightly as she cried, her confusion getting the best of her. After a few minutes, she calmed down and Andrew looked at her and wiped her tears away with his thumbs as he held her face in his hands.

"Is this my room? It looks familiar, but I'm not sure...." Anna asked him in earnest. She saw his heartbreak in his blue eyes as tears began to well up.

"I am so sorry, Anna," he whispered, hugging her tightly again. "This never should have happened to you and we are going to get to the bottom of it," he added, regaining his composure.

"You love me," she stated softly. "I can see it," she added with a little smile.

"Yes," he said with a relieved little laugh. "Yes, Anna. I love you."

"Okay," she said simply, then climbed back into bed. "Let's get some sleep."

Andrew lay next to her with a heavy heart. *What if I can't help her?* he wondered. *What if all of this ends up being for nothing and she's lost forever?*

Chapter Sixteen

Andrew was up before dawn poring over everything they'd gathered about Morgellons over the last few months. He was especially interested in the discovery that there were crystals in the fibers, and he needed to know how to get to the information stored there. He was also particularly disturbed by the fact that the Morgellons fibers seemed to move toward him as he looked at them under the microscope. Was it possible that they could move around freely *within* someone's body?

As he heard Anna walking around the bedroom upstairs, he wondered if she would remember anything this morning. He hoped that she would, but he was mentally and emotionally prepared for her not to. *I just hope that she hangs in there long enough for me to figure out what to do about this....*

"Good morning," Anna said cheerfully as she walked into the kitchen and kissed Andrew on the lips. "What are you doing up so early?" she asked, glancing at his research, which was spread out across the dining room table.

"Just going over all of our research again," he replied. She was acting normal, so he decided to go with it.

"Research on what?" she asked. Andrew's face fell.

"You still don't remember?" he asked. She shook her head and he sighed deeply.

"Okay," he said. "It's hard to describe, but I'll fill you in over breakfast."

"I suppose... does it have something to do with the weird strings coming out of my body? Because I've been trying to figure that one out for a long time...." she trailed off. *At least she remembers having tried to figure it out on her own,* he thought.

"Yes it does, actually," Andrew said. "So you do remember a little bit?"

"A little. I definitely remember us making love last night," she said with a wink, and Andrew just smiled to hide his panic. They hadn't made love that night. He didn't touch her except to comfort her because that would've been completely messed up when she didn't remember him.

∞

"I think we're on our own on this one," Andrew told Casey and Jake softly. "She doesn't remember you, she doesn't remember me, and now she seems to be forming new memories without those things actually happening," he added, fighting the urge to punch a wall in frustration. "At least I hope that's what happening, because if it's something else, that would be even worse."

"What's that supposed to mean?" Casey asked, exchanging a puzzled look with Jake.

"That means if she and I didn't make love last night, then who was she... you know...?" Casey's eyes widened.

"What else can you tell us about last night?" she asked, seriously concerned for her best friend.

"Not much... I mean, she woke up in the middle of the night and sounded like she was talking to someone, but when I woke up to that, I didn't see anyone and she got all freaked out about *me* because she didn't remember me or even her own room."

"Is there anything else you remember? Maybe something she said?" Andrew shook his head and rubbed his forehead with his fingers in frustration. Casey slumped back in her chair, disappointed, but then Andrew abruptly stopped and furrowed his brows.

"You know what," he began slowly. "She did say something. She asked me if I saw the shadow. Not shadow-s, but shadow, singular. I wonder if that has something to do with last night being so pivotal in her memory issues?"

"Maybe," Casey said. "Let's make a note of it and keep it in mind as we try to get her better. I think we need to forget about finding out what this is all about and focus on curing her," she added. "Did you call the douche-bag yet?"

"James? Yea," Andrew said. "I asked him to meet me later today for a drop. When I go, I'll see if I can get anything out of him."

"Good! Maybe he'll be able to shed some light on—"

"I see you're already talking about me," a new voice cut Casey off. Andrew stood defensively.

"What are you doing here?" he asked, keeping his rage bubbling under.

"You wanted to meet... I figured I already know where Anna lives, so why not just drop by?"

Anna stood slightly behind him, smiling.

"He was at the door," she said cheerfully. "He said you were friends and he needed to talk to you about something important." She beamed at Andrew and went back into the living room to sit down and watch TV, holding her mug of coffee.

"We were supposed to meet somewhere *else*," Andrew said through clenched teeth, grabbing James' arm roughly and leading him into the kitchen where the others waited.

"Ah, so this is your little band of would-be heroes, right?" James chuckled. "Just so you all know, we already know exactly what you're up to and it won't work."

"Oh?" Casey asked, getting angry. "And how would you know, jerk?"

"That's not important," James answered. "What *is* important is that you three are on everyone's shit list," he continued, lowering his voice. "You have no idea what you're getting yourselves into and you need to stop before something really terrible happens."

"Something terrible already *is* happening!" Andrew interjected. "Now, if this is for some kind of purpose or cause, then maybe we could understand why Anna's going through such a hard time, but to us – as it stands right now – it's for absolutely *nothing*."

"I see your dilemma, but I also know you don't have clearance, so I can't tell you anything," James said coldly, eyeing the others.

Before anyone could react, Anna appeared behind him out of nowhere with a bookend and hit him in the back of the head with it, hard. James crumpled to the floor and everyone looked at Anna in shock and pleased surprise.

"What are you doing?" Andrew asked in disbelief. "Now he'll definitely be out for blood...." he trailed off as he hurried through the kitchen, rummaging through drawers.

"What are you looking for?" Casey asked.

"Rope! Zip ties! Anything!" Andrew said frantically. Jake stood in shock and watched what was happening, mouth agape. Within seconds, Andrew found a package of zip ties, a wash cloth, and some duct tape to make sure that James wouldn't be able to make too much noise.

"We don't even have a basement," Anna said, smiling. She looked like she was about to lose it. "I don't know what the hell I'm doing at all anymore!" she said loudly, bursting into a fit of hysterical giggles. "I just remembered all of you and him and he pissed me off!" she added.

"Wait, you remembered?" Andrew asked, looking at her as he tightened the zip tie around James' left foot and a chair leg. Anna was still giggling.

"Yes!" she said, and suddenly her laughter faded. "Oh, no...." she said, moving from hysterics to tears in rapid succession. "Oh, my God!" she gasped. "Omigod, omigod, omigod...." Casey rushed to her side just as she plopped down onto the floor, grief-stricken.

"What is it, Anna?" Casey asked as she and the two men exchanged confused looks.

"We didn't make love last night," Anna sobbed with fear and panic clearly evident on her face. "*We* didn't make love last night!" she said more loudly, gesturing wildly between herself and Andrew. Her mind was quickly putting together that she had been violated... from inside of her own mind. One of those creatures had manipulated her mind and set off electrical impulses in her brain that made her think she was making love to Andrew....

"Get his hands zip tied behind the chair," Andrew told Jake as he rushed to Anna's side. He sat on the floor next to her and cradled her in his arms as she sobbed, hysterical.

"One of those... *things*...." she trailed off as memories from the previous night flashed before her eyes, only this time, she didn't see only Andrew... she also saw the red-eyed shadow that had spoken to her.

"What happened?" he asked. "What did it do to you?"

"I—I don't know for sure...."

"Andrew!" Jake shouted from the kitchen where James was flailing his free arm around wildly, trying to grab Jake's shirt. Andrew jumped up and subdued James, then finished zip tying him to the chair. When he got done and things had settled down, Andrew went back to Anna's side.

"Can you tell me what happened?" Andrew asked her again, moving strands of her disheveled brown hair out of her face.

"It... it was like it was in my head with me," she said and let out another sob. From across the room, they all heard James' muffled laughter through his makeshift gag. *Yep, he's still a douche-bag*, Andrew thought as he got up and stalked over to the man to let him talk. He tore off the freshly applied duct tape slowly in hopes that it would hurt more that way. Then he took the washcloth out of James' mouth.

"What's so funny, asshole?" Andrew asked, watching James intently as he licked his lips and worked his jaw to shake off the feeling of being gagged.

"You're too late," he said, still smiling. "It's already started! They're on their way here!"

The four friends exchanged an alarmed and confused look.

"Who?" Andrew asked. This prompted almost hysterical laughter from James. Anna and Casey looked at each other.

"Is he completely insane?" Casey asked Anna, who just shrugged.

"The shadows!" James finally spat out. "They're coming for us! Well... not *all* of us, but at least those who have Morgellons!"

"What?!" Andrew yelled in disbelief. "What are you talking about?!"

"They're kind of like people... but they're *not* people," James continued, calming his laughter. "They're from another *dimension*," he said, and he started laughing again. "I can't believe it actually worked!" he said more or less to himself. "I can't believe they're actually *real!*"

"Well, he's lost it," Jake said, finally snapping out of it with what he thought would be a joke. "What the hell is he going on about?" he asked Andrew. Andrew wore a severe expression on his face as he looked at Anna and went back over to where she sat.

"Are they real, Anna? Did the shadows appear to you last night?" She nodded as a silent tear escaped. "Do you still feel like it's in your head with you?" he asked. She shook her head, no.

"Not right now, but I think the Morgellons fibers have something to do with it being able to do that," she said.

"I think you're right," Andrew said softly. "That's why our next step is to kill whatever fibers are left within your body. What if there are some in your brain and that's how this is all happening and affecting your mind so much?" he blurted out. Anna's eyes widened. She remembered having the same notion not long ago.

"That would make perfect sense. It would also explain how one of them got into my tear duct," she said.

"So maybe the fibers aren't all supposed to come out," Andrew began brainstorming. "Maybe some of them are supposed to make their way into your head to affect the brain in such a way that another consciousness can enter into your mind."

"It sounds crazy," Anna said. "But *this whole thing* is crazy."

"Look at the brains on these nerds!" James said, still in hysterics. It really did seem like he suddenly snapped when he realized the entire mission he was on was real. He must not have believed it before. "They have the technology!" he added. "Those creatures are way beyond us! That's how they got the government to agree to this deal in the first place!" He kept laughing.

"How hard did you hit him in the head?" Andrew asked Anna with a little smile. "He seems to be completely out of it!" Anna smiled back.

"It was just a bookend...."

"Well... as much as I'm proud of you for getting us answers and making sure he isn't such a threat anymore," Andrew began, "I think you may have damaged something in his noggin." Anna frowned.

"How? I don't even hit that hard."

"He could've already had a TBI and you may have exacerbated it by reinforcing more trauma. That's okay, though. He starts spouting this crap anywhere but here, people will think he's crazy anyway."

"Well, but... how are we gonna figure out how to cure Morgellons, or at least keep those shadow things from taking over our bodies? I mean... at first it was like I was just talking to it but then it... touched me without touching me, if that makes sense.... And the next thing I know I think I'm making love to you but really it was the shadow doing something in my head. I can't explain it... it's like I can't even remember body parts, only sensations. Did I talk in my sleep or anything like that?"

Andrew shook his head uncomfortably.

"No, you were sound asleep all night after that incident. No tossing or turning, either."

"So the Morgellons and the shadows must be manipulating people's minds, emotions, consciousness, subconscious...."

"That's the best explanation I've heard so far," Andrew said. "As much as it disturbs and disgusts me to think of some creature from another dimension knocking around in your head and manipulating your control like that... violating you like that...."

"I don't feel so good," Anna said suddenly, turning a shade of green and rushing toward the kitchen sink, where she vomited.

It's worse than rape, she thought and vomited again, turning on the water in the sink so she could run the disposal. Andrew had made his way to her side slowly, waiting for her to finish the bulk of it so that he could rub her back without getting sick himself.

"I feel fucking violated *on the inside,*" Anna said hoarsely after a moment. "Nobody is supposed to be able to get into your *brain...* ever!" she added. Andrew rubbed her back as she swished water around her mouth and then wiped her face with a paper towel.

"I'm so sorry, Anna," he said, trying to comfort her. He didn't know what she was feeling. There were probably only a handful of people in the entire world who knew what Anna was going through, and chances were that most of them wouldn't remember anyway. As Anna turned around, Andrew pulled her into an embrace and she just stayed there quietly for a few moments. She didn't cry anymore.

At least now I know what happened, she thought, letting her fear and shame churn themselves into something more useful: rage.

"How can we kill off the Morgellons fibers?" Anna demanded after a moment of deliberation. She walked over to where James sat, still zip tied to the chair. She glared at him intently for a few moments, her hazel eyes smoldering and seeing into the dark pits of his soul. His expression briefly flashed anxiety, but it was subtle. Only Anna noticed.

She slapped him across the face as hard as she could.

"How can we kill off the fibers?!" she demanded again more loudly as the others watched her, shocked. This was a side of Anna that none of them had ever witnessed before.

James furrowed his brows. "I'm not a doctor, I don't—"

She slapped him again, cutting him off.

"If I have to ask you one more time, I'm cutting off a finger to send to your bosses," she said menacingly. Hatred burned in her eyes and Andrew was worried she might do something she would regret. He pulled her aside for a moment.

"Torture?" he asked her softly. "Is that really the best way to go about this?" he asked. Her eyes softened.

"I don't know," she told him. "But I'm so... fucking... pissed... off!" she said at ascending volume with each word. He hugged her again briefly, then looked at her squarely in the face.

"I know you are. I am, too. But we've got to be smart about this." He paused, gently stroking her shoulders as he watched her anger simmer down a little. "We can test different types of medicine, see if we can kill the fibers off like a parasite."

"Do you think that will cure the disease?" Anna asked. Andrew sighed.

"I don't know. But it might tell us if the fibers are what's giving those things control over your brain." Anna nodded in decisive agreement.

"Okay," she said. "I'm alright with that," she added, calmer now. She looked at James. "What do we do with him?" Andrew thought for a moment. He smiled.

"Maybe he can still do something for us," Andrew said, and approached James. Anna nodded and Casey and Jake rushed to her side to find out what was going on.

"*Jimmy!*" Andrew said, looking at his face. Anna may not have done a ton of damage, but she definitely gave him some bruising and a small cut on his cheek. Andrew smiled despite himself. He knew that what he was about to do might jeopardize everything, but he needed Anna to know the whole truth. The truth he'd been keeping from her the entire time. The truth that would force James to talk.

"What?" James asked, serious now that he realized how angry Anna was. *If she has one of those things in her head and manages to stay herself at the same time, there's no telling what could happen,* he thought.

"I wonder if we could make some kind of deal," he said carefully.

"Why?" James asked with a snort. "What could you possibly have that I want?"

"Let me ask you something," Andrew began, hoping to get across to him but keeping his guard up. The moment of truth was upon him. "Why did you get involved with the BQS in the first place?" Anna, Casey, and Jake just stood across the room, watching and listening.

James sighed. "Really? This is how you want to play it?" He gave Andrew a cruel smile. "No wonder you haven't figured it all out yet," he added.

"Oh, but that's where you're wrong," Andrew said, knowing full well that what he was about to disclose could potentially kill his relationship with Anna. Anna and Casey shot each other a confused look. He'd been dreading this moment for a while. But since the opportunity for full disclosure hadn't come up the night they told

Casey what was happening, he felt that this was his time to come clean. He just couldn't decide what he was more nervous about... the BQS coming after him or Anna no longer being in love with him.

"What's that supposed to mean?" James asked, looking skeptical.

"That means that I know a bit more than what I've let on," he said. Anna's eyes widened and she felt her heart skip a beat. The rage that had cooled just moments before came bubbling to the surface again, but she stood there stiffly, waiting to hear him out. *No wonder he's been so calm,* she thought. *And no wonder he seemed like he was hiding something!*

"Oh, really. Hate to break it to ya, but I don't believe that for a second. You're full of shit!" James spat.

"I happen to know that you work for a special government arm of the BQS called The Association. You're an enforcer. Bottom of the food chain. You're not cleared to know nearly as much as you want us to think you are, and in fact, your clearance doesn't cover some of the stuff you just told us. You're in violation of your terms, and since you shared classified information with civilians, you could be tried for treason. However, since The Association and the BQS isn't even supposed to exist, it wouldn't be an actual trial and you know what they're more likely to do to you instead."

"How do you know all that?" James asked incredulously, clutching to the last bits of skepticism he had.

"I know because I'm in a government branch of the BQS called Fragments. No one knows we exist, either, especially the rest of the organization and the government. We work in the shadows. But I promise you, I have higher clearance than you do and *I* didn't even know some of the stuff you told us today, so I thank you for that."

"You're so full of shit!" James yelled defiantly. "I've never even heard of you! Or your stupid division! I would've known about something like that!"

"You don't know about us because we don't technically exist. That was done on purpose. Why do you think the BQS made it look like I died only to certain people?" Andrew remained calm and calculating throughout the conversation. Anna wasn't sure whether to be angry or afraid, but she was a little of both. Casey and Jake watched the conversation play out with wide eyes, unsure of how to respond to any of it. It *was* a real conspiracy.

"So, the question that you really need to consider isn't whether I'm lying or not," Andrew continued. "The question you should really be asking yourself is whether you want to take the risk of being punished for treason, whatever that may entail, or whether you'd rather help us figure out how to get rid of these fibers in a human body."

With that, Andrew stood up calmly, went around the kitchen island, and poured himself a glass of wine. He gestured to his three shocked friends and offered them a glass, too. They all accepted and drank in silence, waiting for James to mull over what Andrew had said, and mulling it over themselves, too.

Anna was in shock. No... she was angry and felt a bit used. Of course she'd rather side with Andrew than with one of those shadow beings, but she didn't know if he had more secrets. So she was also hurt. *Too many conflicting emotions,* she thought, chugging her wine and filling the glass back up immediately. Andrew put a hand gently on her shoulder and looked into her eyes intently.

"This doesn't change how I feel about you," he said. She didn't know how to reply or whether it was safe to open her mouth and try to form words, so she only trusted herself to nod her head. "We can talk more about it later, after James here tells us how to cure you, since he seems to know so damn much about everything."

James groaned in frustration, having thought about Andrew's compromise.

"I really don't think I should tell you any more than I already have," he said.

"I guess you and I will have to find new accommodations, then, because I'm not gonna leave you a choice in the matter. Or I can just turn you over right now. That's up to you. Have you heard of a man by the name of Paragon?" James' eyes widened. "You know, he's the second number on my speed dial. Anna's the first," he said, taking a second to wink at her. *He is* thoroughly *enjoying this,* Anna thought, slightly disturbed but also flattered and a little turned on.

"Okay," James said after a few seconds. "F-fine," he stammered. "I'll tell you what I know, but don't turn me in. That fucker is completely out-of-his-mind scary," he said.

"See? That's better," Andrew said with his radiant smile. He pulled out a chair and sat on it backwards so he was facing James. "Now, let me ask you the question again," he said calmly. "How can we kill off the Morgellons fibers?"

"They have medicine to do that," James began. "I don't know exactly where it is or how it works, but they have medicine for it. I overheard them talking and there's nothing on earth that can treat it, so they created some with the help of the other beings in case something went wrong."

"How much of this medicine is there?" Andrew asked.

"There's a formula... and I think a couple hundred cures already created. They gave us the disease, but it only took with a certain number of people. The last estimate was at fifty thousand."

"And you don't know where they keep it?" Andrew asked. James shook his head. "How about a best guess?" he asked.

"Best guess would be BQS headquarters," James replied. "That's in Seattle, downtown, but there's no sign or anything. I don't even know if they're listed anywhere. The building is just office space. One of the skyscrapers in the city. The BQS is on the top floor."

"Good to know," Andrew said. "Do you happen to have an address for this building?" James shook his head.

"I've never been there, but Plaza Square has been mentioned."

"That narrows it down to two buildings," Anna chimed in. She turned her laptop to face Andrew, who nodded his head in approval.

"Alright. So we need alien medicine. Why do we need alien medicine? Why does nothing on earth work? It's like a parasite, isn't it?" Andrew dreaded the idea of breaking into that office building. They'd have to case it and determine the best plan of action.

"Because it isn't just a parasite," James started, but then paused. "It's apparently so much more than that. And they aren't aliens, they're interdimensional."

"Explain the parasite."

"I... I'm not sure if I can or if I even understand it myself," he said wearily.

"Try."

"It's technology... at least part of it is. *Their* tech, not ours, although they may or may not be introducing us to it once they cross over," he said, still in a bit of disbelief about the whole thing being true.

"So it isn't just a worm," Andrew said. "Damn. If it were it would be easier to get rid of. What else?"

179

"They use it to collect information. I don't know how it works, but that's why they pay out so much when people bring them samples; the information helps them determine the best way to cross over."

"I thought they were just sending their consciousness into a human body?" Andrew asked. James let out a short, cynical laugh.

"If you want to believe that," he stated.

"What do you mean?"

"I don't know if this is true or not, but if they can collect information like that about the human body and probably even our atmosphere and everything that exists on earth, in our dimension, why would they need all that if they're just taking over human bodies? Humans are acclimatized already. Think about it. The way they're saying they'll do it only works for a small population from their... world. There could be something going on behind the scenes over there that will enable them to save their entire species. Which this way does not."

"And they called *me* a conspiracy nut," Andrew mumbled. "If that's the case, we have a much bigger problem on our hands," he continued, looking at the others. Glancing back at James, he asked, "And why the fuck would you help them do something like this? Do you just enjoy being a dick?" James looked down somberly.

"By the time I figured out what was really going on, I was in way too deep," he admitted. "If this were the kind of job you could just quit, I would have. But it isn't. Instead, they made sure I didn't have anything left to quit *for*."

"Alright," Andrew said, accepting his answer. "I guess that means we have some work to do. Do you have any idea who worked on the cure for Morgellons on this side? I'm assuming they can't send anything physical to earth as of yet, so who worked on it? Any ideas?"

"It was Dr. Schwartz, if that's even his real name. I worked his security detail so he could do some work in a weird research facility in Tacoma somewhere. Something about genetics...."

Anna interjected. "Um... I know Dr. Schwartz," Anna realized with wide eyes. "He was at the lab...."

"What?" James interrupted. "You've been there? What were you doing there?!"

"Hey, I'll ask the questions," Andrew said loudly.

"Dude, I work there," Jake said at the same time, then wished he hadn't, especially when Andrew, Anna, *and* Casey all gave him a disapproving look. "Shit. Sorry!"

"You made it a lot further than I would've given you credit for," James remarked, genuinely surprised but still sounding snarky.

"Time for the asshole tied to the chair to shut up!" Andrew snapped, walking over and replacing James' gag roughly. He went back and returned his attention to Anna and the others. "Are you telling me we've already met this genetic magician?" he asked. Anna nodded.

"Sophia... the little girl I give art lessons to? That's his daughter," she said, shaking her head. "This *can't* be a coincidence...."

"Let's go talk to him," Casey said. "What's the worst that could happen? He kicks us out. We aren't doing anything wrong by having a conversation," she added, hoping that her logic would make sense to everyone like it did to her. She was sick of feeling like a criminal. Although now she was feeling a little more like a spy, and that was much worse.

"That's what we'll do," Andrew stated, "but not all of us. In case something happens, we have to split up," he said. The four of them exchanged a glance, dreading who would wind up stuck babysitting James.

"I know nobody wants to stay here, but someone has to watch him until we're sure we have everything he can tell us," Andrew said sympathetically. James groaned exaggeratedly from across the kitchen island.

"Maybe we can make our case better if I go with you," Anna offered a little hesitantly. "I do have the disease," she added, glancing sidelong at Casey, who was smiling and shot Jake a quick glance of her own.

"Sure," Casey agreed happily. Jake was a little less excited about it, but he agreed since being associated with this conversation would absolutely get him fired if they got escorted out.

"Then it's settled," Andrew said, smiling at Anna and taking her hand. "We're gonna go speak with Mr. Genetic Engineer."

James stayed silent in concentration. He'd managed to grab a kitchen knife and was slowly but steadily working on the zip ties behind his back.

Chapter Seventeen

"I can't believe this is really happening," Anna said softly as Andrew drove them to the Tacoma research facility.

"I know what you mean," Andrew said. "It was like that for me for a while, too," he added, reigniting the topic of his deception.

"Yea... speaking of which," she said, "why have you been keeping all of this from me for so long? You know I hate secrets." She wasn't angry anymore, just overwhelmed and nervous about going to speak to Dr. Schwartz. How deep did his involvement run? How much did he know? Did what Sophia told her about him doing something to her code have a connection to Morgellons?

"I've wanted to tell you so many times," Andrew said, placing his free hand on her thigh as he drove. "I was just torn because of threats from James and what might happen to you if I did tell you. This is way bigger than we thought," he added, sounding like he was in disbelief himself.

"I know it is, Andrew," she said with a sigh, intertwining her fingers with his on her thigh. "What are we gonna do if James was right and they try to save their entire species by crossing over physically? I'm not some kind of hero or spy or whatever you guys call yourselves.... I'm scared."

"They call us Interdimensional Liaison Operatives," he said softly. "ILOs. We're meant to communicate indirectly – some directly – and follow whatever orders come down to collect samples, observe, and report. And I know you're scared. But Anna, we are *so* close to curing you, and we can handle whatever comes next *together*. You and me... and Jake and Casey, if they're up to it." He let out a little chuckle, as did Anna.

"I just hate being so nervous," she said, heaving another big sigh and shaking her head as if to make her feelings fall away.

"I know, baby," he said sympathetically. "But right now, we're just going to see Dr. Schwartz. With any luck, he'll be sympathetic to you and has a solution we can use. If he's the one who created the cure for Morgellons, he may have kept the formula and he may have even made a few extras just in case. Everything else is still up in the air because we don't know what's going to happen yet, okay?"

"Okay," she said. She took a controlled breath in, then exhaled slowly through her mouth, imagining all of her anxiety and worry leaving her body.

"I love you, Anna," Andrew said as he gave her hand a quick squeeze.

"I love you, too," she replied, still trying to exhale the flurry of butterflies in her stomach. *Why can't I shake off this dread in the pit of my stomach?*

∞

"It's been great chatting with you two," James said happily as he finished zip tying Casey to one of the kitchen chairs. "I know that's an unpleasant way to sit, but someone is bound to find you sooner or later, right? Worst case, when your bodies start smelling bad." He let out a short laugh and left Anna's house, wondering if he should've killed them instead.

As he approached his car, he made sure his sidearm was loaded and tucked it into its holster. He hopped into his car and peeled out, speeding to try to get to the lab before the other two clowns did. *I should've killed them both when I had the chance....*

He turned the music up.

∞

"We'd just like to talk to you for a few minutes, Dr. Schwartz," Anna pleaded, rolling up both of her sleeves. "Please?" Dr. Schwartz's features softened as he saw her Morgellons-riddled arms.

"My heart goes out to you... it really does, but I simply can't help you," he said and turned to walk away.

"We know about the BQS," Andrew piped up softly. Dr. Schwartz stopped in his tracks and turned back to face the couple as he sighed. "We also know that hiring Anna for your daughter's art lessons was no coincidence," Andrew added. Anna kept her expression as blank as she could, hoping that particular speculation was correct.

"How do you know about the BQS?" Dr. Schwartz asked, motioning for them to follow him. They walked with him to his office two floors up from where they'd run into him.

"I work for them... indirectly," Andrew said carefully after they all stepped into the doctor's office. "We know you created a cure for Morgellons and all we ask is that you help Anna," Andrew said. "You obviously want to, and what's one person compared to fifty thousand?" he added, seeing that the doctor was truly torn.

"You don't understand," Dr. Schwartz began, shaking his head. "This is so much more complicated than you know," he added.

"What about Sophia?" Anna asked. "What will she do when she realizes that I'm not me anymore? And she's sharp.... There's no way that this will happen without her noticing something's going on. You already know how close she and I are. Then what?"

Dr. Schwartz squeezed the bridge of his nose under his glasses and closed his eyes. Anna and Andrew stayed quiet for a moment. They watched as the doctor pulled a file and a small vial out of a desk drawer.

Before Anna could even smile, the door flew open violently.

"Get down!" Andrew yelled and the three of them hit the floor as shots were fired from the doorway. Thinking fast, Andrew made his way toward the inward-opening door and kicked it, throwing off James' balance. Anna hid behind the desk with the doctor, who was bleeding profusely from his stomach as he handed Anna the file and the medicine.

Andrew was on his feet in a flash, trying to wrestle the gun from James, who managed to graze Andrew's arm with a bullet. Anna held the doctor's head in her arms as he tried to whisper something to her.

"Anna.... Please take care of my girl... the cure is.... hidden in... So...phia...." was all he managed before the light left his eyes.

Andrew had managed to disarm James and knock him unconscious, so the barrage of gunfire ceased. Anna found herself cradling the doctor's head in her arms, weeping softly with her hands covered in blood as Andrew made his way to her quickly. The entire encounter had happened in seconds, so he knew that they had to move fast.

Andrew grabbed the file and the vial of medicine from the doctor's lifeless hands and hid them on his person just before the building's security detail burst into the office, guns trained on Andrew and Anna. Andrew raised his hands in surrender as he gestured toward the doctor's lifeless form on the floor. They saw James' unconscious body and stepped over it, the scene making it obvious that he had been the shooter.

"Are you okay?" one of the guards asked Andrew, who nodded. Helping Anna get up, she just wept in his arms, traumatized and covered in Dr. Schwartz's blood.

"Don't go too far," the guard told Andrew. "They're gonna want a statement." Andrew nodded, leading Anna away from the macabre scene.

∞

"We know this is unpleasant, but is there anything else you can tell us?" one of the guards asked.

"We've been over this five times already," Andrew stated, irritated at their line of questioning toward Anna. "The shooter came in and opened fire. No one knows why or what happened. We were just here to talk to Dr. Schwartz about his daughter, Sophia, who takes art lessons from Anna."

"He asked me to take care of her," Anna said softly, wiping away a stray tear. "He wants me to adopt Sophia. But how am I supposed to tell her that... that her father is...." Anna began sobbing again.

"Do any of you know where Sophia is?" Andrew asked the guard. He pulled his sleeve down over the bandage they'd put on his arm.

"Your guess is as good as mine," the guard replied. "Alright, look. If that's all that happened and this was a random crime, everything will be fine." He paused and they watched some of the guards take James away with his hands secured behind his back. James looked over his shoulder at Anna and smiled disturbingly.

"However," he continued, "if the man we have in custody says otherwise, we may need to contact you again." He produced a business card and handed it to Anna. "If you think of anything that might be relevant, no matter how small a detail it may seem, please give me a call."

With that, he walked away and the crew that was there to investigate continued taking photos and taping off the doctor's office. None of them were actual police officers. Andrew put his arm around

Anna and guided her out of the building. She was in shock and he had no idea how quickly she would snap out of it, if at all.

But at least they had a cure for her now.

∞

Anna stared out the open window of the passenger side of the car, letting the breeze cool her grief-stricken face. Anna assumed that the BQS didn't want anyone to get wind of their organization or the tragedy that had occurred, especially the press. That was the only logical explanation for there not being any real police or EMTs there.

Andrew had realized quickly that Jake and Casey may be dead or in danger, so he knew they had to get out of there fast. Neither Jake nor Casey were answering their phones, and Anna was worried, helplessly willing the car to go faster and her friends to be okay. She was also exhausted, and definitely couldn't handle any more tragedy that day.

Just thinking about it made her bust into sobs again, and Andrew placed his hand on her thigh to comfort her. His feelings were a tangled mess he'd have to work hard to sort through, especially since he was glad that they'd at least gotten the formula for the cure as well as one vial for Anna. More than anything, he was pissed off that James was such a psycho and that the bastard might have also killed Jake and Casey.

He pushed down harder on the accelerator.

About the Author

Jennifer-Crystal Johnson is originally from Germany, but was raised in numerous places. She has published one novella under her former last name, The Outside Girl: Perception is Reality (Publish America, 2005 - out of print), a poetry book, Napkin Poetry (Broken Publications, 2010), and a collection of poetry, art, and prose called Strangers with Familiar Faces (Broken Publications, 2011). More recently, Jen published If You're Human Don't Open the Door (Broken Publications, 2012) and Our Capacity for Evil (Broken Publications, 2015), both collections of short horror stories. Her poem, Yin & Yang, was featured on Every Writer's Resource's Poem a Day site, along with two other poems. One of her short stories, The Huntress, was featured in Zombie Coffee Press (no longer online), and another short horror story, Simple Truth, was published on Every Writer's Resource. Her poetry has appeared in various anthologies. She currently works as a freelance writer and editor as well as helping other authors self-publish their own books.

She lives in the Pacific Northwest with her three kids, three cats, and their puppy, Thor. Her domestic violence anthology can be found at www.SoulVomit.com and her publishing company is Broken Publications. She recently began creating video tutorials about how to self-publish, which can be found at No Bull Self-Publishing. Last but not least, she recently started an anthology called Beneath the Veil of Night. Submission guidelines and links for the first three themes can be found on the Submissions page at www.BrokenPublications.com.

Other Books by Jennifer-Crystal Johnson

Our Capacity for Evil, Broken Publications, 2015.
Short horror stories (people & psychological).

If You're Human Don't Open the Door, Broken Publications, 2012.
Short horror stories (creatures).

The Ten Pillars of a Happy Relationship, Broken Publications, 2014.
Personal development & relationships.

Strangers with Familiar Faces, Broken Publications, 2011.
Poetry & digital art.

Napkin Poetry, Broken Publications, 2010.
Poetry.

Soul Vomit: Domestic Violence Aftermath, Broken Publications, 2014.
Anthology: poetry, short stories, art, photography, essays, prose by various contributors. Edited and prepared for publication by Jennifer-Crystal Johnson.

Soul Vomit: Beating Domestic Violence, Broken Publications, 2012.
Anthology: poetry, short stories, art, photography, essays, prose by various contributors. Edited and prepared for publication by Jennifer-Crystal Johnson.

Did You Love This Book?

If so, please leave a short review on Amazon! It doesn't have to be much; just a simple star rating and a quick sentence or two saying that you enjoyed it.

Leaving reviews doesn't just help authors improve their work, it helps readers like you find the best new books and discover new authors you love.

Something as simple as:

> I read this book as the first of a series and really enjoyed it! I highly recommend that you check it out.

... will do perfectly =). (Feel free to copy and paste for your convenience!)

Ready to leave your review now? Go to:

http://amzn.to/1U4yLSp

Made in the USA
San Bernardino, CA
17 March 2016